THE GREAT GREEN APPLE WAR

THE GREAT GREEN APPLE WAR

BARBARA KLIMOWICZ

DRAWINGS BY
LEE J. AMES

ABINGDON PRESS

Nashville   New York

Klimowicz, Barbara.
   The great green apple war.
   SUMMARY: On the night of his initiation into the enviable "orchard gang,"
an eleven-year-old realizes the inevitability of change in one's life and the need
to adjust one's goals accordingly.
   I. Ames, Lee J., illus.   II. Title.
PZ7.K679Gr   [Fic]   72-6224
ISBN 0-687-15684-X

Weekly Reader Children's Book Club Edition

For
my sister, Rosemary,
who remembers the orchard

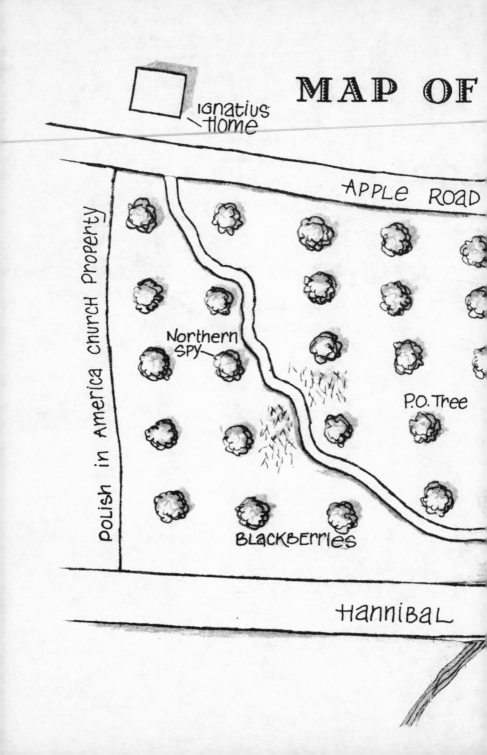

THE ORCHARD

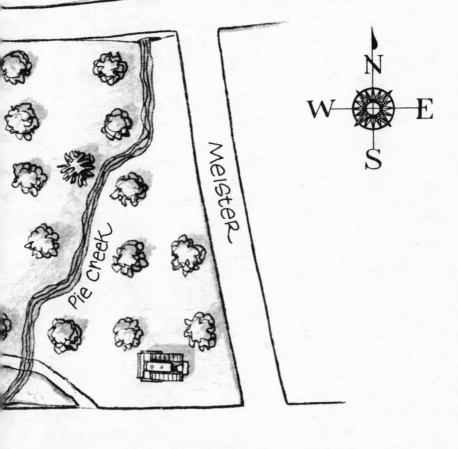

culvert

Meister

Pie Creek

PICKLY WICKLY

N
W E
S

Tonight is the night I must sleep in the orchard, and nobody knows it but me. Ta is chewing a toothpick out on the front porch and rattling his newspaper into the right shape for reading. Ma is watering her fern in the dining room. Felicia and Irka and Reka are making like hens over the supper dishes —cluckety-cluckety-cluck.

It is awful to have three older sisters. They keep thinking this house is a nest and I am an egg. That is to say, they sit on me. They tell me not to do this and not to do that. They tell me to put on a sweater and tie my shoes. Peck-peck-peck. It is like having three extra mothers. Oh, the poor luck I have to be born a boy in a family of girls. And worse it is to be born very last. Felicia is already nineteen, Irka eighteen, and Reka sixteen. They have been flapping their wings at me ever since I was born—that is to say for eleven years. I guess they don't know I've hatched and need to flap my own wings a little. I guess that's why I go to the orchard all the time—to flap.

And tonight I must sleep in the orchard alone. It is part of getting to be one of the Willow Tree Gang. It is what they call initiation. I must tell Ta and Ma and Felicia and Irka and Reka. And it is a very hard thing to do. I must tell them in such a way that they will let me go. That is a very, very hard thing to do. I think that only Ta will understand. That will be him and me against Ma and Felicia and Irka and Reka. And I'm not even sure of Ta. Sometimes when his feet hurt and the day has been like an oven and his hands are blistered from the hot hose at the rubber factory, he is on nobody's side. But still, he is my best bet. I will start with Ta.

I sit beside him on the porch swing, and he rumbles in his throat because I have made the printing in his newspaper bounce. "Ta," I say.

"Hmm," he says, his eyes still following the print.

"I have to sleep in the orchard tonight," I say. With Ta you say what you say. You don't sneak up on him with hints and pleases.

Ta lets the newspaper cave in against his chest. "How old are you?" he asks.

"Eleven."

"Stand up." I try to stand tiptoe inside my sneakers where it won't show. Ta nods his head. "You are old enough and big enough. If you think you are brave enough and smart enough, you will sleep in the orchard." He lifts the newspaper again. That is that. Now there are two on my side—Ta and me. I go to the dining room.

"Ma, I think I'll camp out tonight."

"Camp out?" With Ma you have to explain things.

"Yes, sleep outdoors, Ma."

11

"You sleep outdoors? What's the matter the bed, the good big bed all your own and the good big bedroom by yourself? For this your sisters, they sleep all crowded in one room?" Ma shakes her head in disbelief. I follow her to the kitchen.

"I like the room, Ma. I like the bed. I am a lucky boy to have a whole room to myself and a bed. But tonight I have to sleep in the orchard."

"The orchard yet! And what is this *have to?*"

I try to think what to say. How can I explain initiation to Ma, if she cannot even understand sleeping outdoors?

"He shouldn't go, Ma," says Reka. "Those kids in the orchard are bad, real bad!"

"That Jack Campanelli carries a knife," says Irka.

"Bums, maybe, sleep there at night," says Felicia to me. "Wouldn't you be afraid?" Suddenly the kitchen is quiet. The dishes stop clattering. The hot water stops gushing into the sink. Everybody stops talking and looks at me. That is the question I can't answer—am I afraid. I don't know why my heart is pounding. Is it because the hands of the kitchen clock are eating chunks out of my time and I will be late? Or is it because I do not know the night orchard or how far the Willow Gang will test my courage?

"If you are afraid, Ignatius," says Ma, "why do you wish to go?"

"Please, Ma," I say, and I feel tears lying hot behind my eyeballs. I am ashamed because in the orchard I am known as a tough cookie. It is queer that at home I am a little boy and in the orchard I am a tough cookie. Suddenly Ta looms in the kitchen doorway.

"He has to go. It is part of growing up for a boy. It is like going to school and studying History or Spelling. Ignatius must go to the orchard and study Afraid." Ta returns to the porch.

It is settled then. When Ta talks like that, everyone knows it is settled.

"There's an old quilt in the attic, Ig," says Felicia. "I'll get it."

"I'm packing you some cookies," says Irka. "You'll get hungry."

"I'll put some milk in a jar," says Reka.

Ma looks at me a long time. She shakes her head sadly. "You get big. I keep thinking you are a little duffer. You'll be home for breakfast, yes? I'll fix you potato *placki*." She smiles, and now I know it is all right with Ma.

Felicia makes a bundle out of the food and the old quilt and follows me down the stairs to the cellar landing before she puts it in my arms.

"I'll leave the backdoor unlocked," she says quietly, "just in case you want to come home early."

My throat is stuck shut and I can't even say thanks. I know I won't be using the unlocked door, but it would be good to say thanks anyhow. I bolt out into the near-night and race behind the garage, where I stuff the bundle behind the smokehouse. I cannot take sissy things to the orchard. I can take only this tough cookie that I am.

Now I must split like the wind. I race across the dark yard, jump the ditch, and pound down Apple Road. I feel Ta's eyes from the porch, like a hand on my shoulder, until I jump the other ditch into the orchard and start zigzagging among the apple trees.

The branches of the Old Willow rise high against the darkish sky. The twigs and little leaves make a pattern like the lace Ma is tatting for the new altar cloth. But I do not need the leaf-lace to guide me to the meeting place. The orchard I know like a book—like Father Janowicz knows the Holy Biblja.

They are waiting at the foot of the Willow Tree. They have ladies' stockings pulled over their faces. If they think to scare me this way, I guess they do— that is to say a little bit. I know who each one is, all right. The tall one is Bean. The short one is Chunk. The one who snickers is Willy. And Jack is the one who hisses, "Shut up!"

So I know who they are. But tonight I don't know what they are. That is the bit that scares me. If they are what they are in the daylight, then I am not afraid. I know their daytime selves. But if they are different at night behind the tight nylon that mashes their noses and twists their mouths and makes them eyeless, then maybe I will be afraid.

They don't talk. They frisk me. When they find I have brought nothing, they point to the rope ladder that leads to the wooden platform in the Willow high above our heads. I know that up there is where I will spend the night. This I know from the note I found this afternoon nailed to the trunk of the Post Office Tree.

I climb the ladder clumsily. Willy snickers again. Many times have I watched the Gang scurry up and down this private ladder like squirrels. It looks easy when you are spying from Tree Cave Number One or from behind a thick stand of cattails by the creek. But doing it the first time is not an easy thing.

When at last I reach the top and crawl onto the floorboards of the treehouse, I turn to loosen the slip-knots that fasten the ladder in place. It is hard to loosen them in the dark, and Jack hisses more than once before I am able to drop the ladder to the ground. Jack snatches it up, and the four of them race away. I watch and listen until they disappear among the apple trees.

Now a prisoner I am. Felicia has left the backdoor unlocked for nothing. I cannot go home even if I wish. The platform is high, and jumping into the darkness below is not a thing a smart cookie would do. Besides, I *want* to be where I am. From the time I was no taller than some of the orchard weeds, I knew that I wanted to be in the Willow Gang. I wanted to sit in the Willow Tree high above the Apple Kingdom and feel power. Now here I am. The power I do not yet feel. But it will come, I suppose. I move back from the edge of the platform and sit hugging my knees.

It is a moony night, and I am glad. The orchard around me is like a 3-D map. The shaggy old heads of the apple trees glitter silver. Ta says this is a very old orchard, maybe seventy-five or eighty years old. The trees have grown big and crooked. They have become their own bosses. No one comes to trim them or spray them or pick their wormy fruit. They stand in their rows as they have stood since they were planted. Ta says they could never pass inspection in anybody's army. They couldn't even belong to the union at the rubber factory. They are sloppy. Some of their branches sag almost to the ground, making cave-like places for orchard spy games.

The orchard fills half a city block, and houses have grown up nearly all around it—tall, skinny, dark brick houses that look all alike except for house numbers and maybe an awning here and a pot of petunias there.

The orchard rests on a longish slope of land. At the high end is the Polish-in-America Church property. Apple Road runs along one side of the orchard and Hannibal along the other. At the low end of the orchard is Meister Street. Some people say that it is a Mister Meister who owns the orchard. I say that maybe it is a Mr. Apple or a Mr. Hannibal. Who knows? Maybe even a Mister Ignatius Zaska—that's me. Whenever I say that, Jack says, "Hah!" and spits on the ground close to my sneakers. For the most part, though, the kids who play here do not ask who owns the orchard. Asking could turn up an owner. We do not want to see NO TRESPASSING signs in our kingdom.

I look down over the edge of the platform to see if

I can see Pie Creek. It isn't much of a creek, but enough to feed the old Willow. Enough to wade in. Enough to catch tadpoles in. Enough to form ice on winter days. From my high perch I can see only a small shining blob of it through the leaves. But that blob holds the moon. I can look up and see the moon. I can look down into the water and see the moon. It gives me a good feeling. I think I am not afraid at all. I guess, if Ma could ask me this very minute if I am afraid of the orchard, I could answer truthfully, "Ma, I am not afraid."

I lie on my back and look up through the black leaf-lace to the blue-black sky and the stars plunked here and there. I should be one happy cookie. For six years I have played in the orchard and dreamed of being big enough and tough enough to join the Willow Gang. For six years my heart beat faster whenever I saw the Willow Tree, and my mouth got dry at the thought of climbing the rope ladder. Now here I am. I should be one happy cookie. But suddenly I am not.

It is a funny thing that now I am not happy. At first it puzzles me. After awhile I know what is the trouble. Seeds. Seeds of worry planted in my brain. I do not understand why things that are little and laughed at in the daytime, start taking root and growing big in the night. Take the ghost of Mister Meister. When Chunk told Curly and me about the ghost, we whooped and hollered. When Bean told us that poisonous snakes live in a hole in the Willow trunk, we said, "Yeah, man, and poisonous bunny rabbits live in the blackberry bushes!" When Willy told us about the Thing with green eyes and hot breath, we said, "Hah!" and we found an empty Listerine bottle in a trash can. We tied it to a limb of the Post Office Tree with a note—TELL THE THING WITH GREEN EYES TO GARGLE. When Jack talked about the red-headed eye-pecker that flies at night, Curly winked at me. We didn't laugh just then because Jack gets fierce when he's laughed at. But when we were alone later, eating jelly bread on my front steps, we laughed ourselves sick. Curly said, "It's a big bunch of baloney! It's initiation propaganda. They think they can scare us! Hah!"

I said, "Hah!" too. But right now in the night alone I don't say, "Hah!" I don't say anything. I just think. About ghosts and snakes and eye-peckers and bums and Things. And I keep wondering if the Gang is coming back to heckle me.

I wish Curly were here. Curly is my best friend. He lives on the Polish-in-America Church property with Father Janowicz. Father Janowicz is his uncle. Curly calls him Uncle Father.

I can see the church bell tower even though it's dark. And that round thing must be the new God window above the High Altar. If Curly had his light on, I could see his bedroom window in the manse. I wonder if he is sleeping or awake. Maybe he is thinking about me up here in the Willow Tree. Maybe he is worrying about tomorrow night when it will be his turn to sleep in the orchard alone.

I wish Curly were here. If Curly were here, we could push back the night with jokes and laughing. We could throw all the seeds of worry into Pie Creek and watch them disappear into the moon. Maybe.

What's that! I hear something! Probably just a

19

mouse or a rabbit or a frog or . . . No, it's bigger. And it's getting closer! Maybe it's the Willow Gang coming back to haunt me. Hah! It sure couldn't be an eye-pecker or a-a-a g-g-ghost or a-a-

"Psst! Hey, Ig!"

"Curly! Is that you?"

"Naw! I'm a Thing with green eyes and hot breath."

Big laugh-bubbles explode from my mouth and bounce against the stars.

"Shhh," warns Curly. "The Gang might be around here!" I slap my hand over my mouth, but the laugh bubbles keep jerking around inside me. It's a funny thing, those laugh bubbles. They almost feel like cry bubbles. My throat aches from trying to keep them quiet.

"I've got a rope, Ig."

"Hey, neat, Curly," I whisper. "Toss it here."

The rope snakes up to meet me, and I grab its tail. I tie it good and tight where the rope ladder was fastened before.

"Are you coming down or me up?" asks Curly.

"I'd better stay up here in case the Gang comes nosing around."

"Yeah. Well, there's nothing says I can't pay a visit."

"Sure thing. And if they come, you can lie down flat and they won't even know you're up here."

The rope begins to creak and the platform jiggle as Curly shinnies upward. When I see his hand grabbing the edge of the platform, I haul him up. He lies there for a minute panting. Then he stands and looks around.

"Hey, this is neat, Ig. You can see everything from up here."

"It's because the moon's so bright."

"Yeah." Curly turns slowly, looking in all directions, and I know his heart has a finger. It's pointing to all the parts of the orchard that are special. I don't even have to look to know what he's naming to himself—Patch Path, the Northern Spy, the blackberry bushes, Tree Cave Number One, the Post Office Tree, Pie Creek, the culvert—

"Hey, Ig."

"What?"

"I can see that bulldozer. I wonder where it came from." Curly sits down beside me. "Sure is mysterious," he adds. "Not a sign of it in the orchard yesterday, then here it was today. And where were we when it came? Why didn't we hear a ruckus or something? Why do you think it's here, Ig?"

I try to put my mind on the mysterious bulldozer. But it's like putting chocolate sauce on an ice cream ball. It just slips off and lies in a puddle in the bottom of the dish. My mind is a puddle. It doesn't want to think. It doesn't want to wonder. It doesn't want to worry. It just wants to be a puddle.

And then it seems like I am leaning over and looking at my reflection in the puddle. I see my face, but it isn't my tough-cookie eleven-year-old face, and it isn't now, in the Willow Tree, being initiated. It's a long time ago, the very first day I stepped into the orchard.

3

It was my fifth birthday that day. I had been itching to visit the orchard ever since I learned to walk. But the orchard was a forbidden land. It's funny how forbidden things and forbidden places stay forever in your head. Even at night in your dreams.

I think the whole year before I was five I stood in the ditch, the ditch beside Apple Road. That was as near the orchard as Ma would allow me. Like a magnet the orchard was. And I could have been Ma's steel tatting hook. I was pulled and pulled and pulled by the orchard. But Ma and Felicia and Irka and Reka were magnets, too. And they pulled and pulled and pulled me away from the orchard. There I was, caught at the edge of the road in a tug-of-war.

But the day I turned five was different. Ma had promised I could cross Apple Road by myself. Ma had promised I could eat lunch with Curly under one of the orchard trees. I had never crossed Apple Road before except attached to someone's hand. And then it was for the going to church, or once in awhile to play with Curly in the manse, quietly, of course, so as not to disturb Father Janowicz at his prayers.

This was a July day, sunny and hot. Ma had made potato *placki* for my breakfast. While I ate, I watched Felicia stirring up a *baba* cake for the five candles.

"A *baba* cake is a woman cake," said Felicia, punching down the dough.

"But I am a boy. I want a boy cake, not a woman cake."

"Silly, it is only called woman because it is baked in this funny round pan that shapes the cake like a woman's skirt. Don't worry, Ignatius. It will taste better than a woman's skirt."

"You be proud," said Ma. "Only a Polish boy gets a *baba* cake."

"But I am an American boy," I said.

"Yes, but Polish is in your blood. That's good to remember." Ma rumpled my hair.

"Where is my lunch?" I asked.

"Here, Mr. Big Boy," said Ma, handing me a sack. "I've fixed you an American lunch." Her eyes laughed. "Peanut butter." She handed me the sack. "How will you cross road?" she asked for the millionth time.

"Stop, look, and listen," I said in a sing-song voice.

"You're a good boy," smiled Ma. "My! Five years old yet!"

The minute I opened the front door and stepped onto the porch I knew that something was different. Right away I knew it wasn't good. The smell hit me first. And then my eyes saw it—the black runny river that was Apple Road. Every summer the City oiled the gravel roads within the City limits. In past

summers the coming of the big oil truck had been a big thing. Its slow trip down Apple Road, gushing oil from the row of faucets in the back, had been almost as good as a parade. But on this special day, seeing the oil was like a bee sting or a thorn in my toe. My eyes filled with tears. After all, I was only five. I was not the tough cookie I am today. Today I am like a ginger snap—hard as nails and spicy as heck. Way back then I was just a little vanilla wafer.

I walked slowly to the ditch. The oil truck was disappearing around the corner and before me was the wide ribbon of black goo. I knew Ma would never let me cross even though it was my birthday. At least three or four days it would take for the oil to soak the road. Maybe longer. Until then, people and pets and even cars would stay away. The cars would park on other streets or stay in garages. Of course, some crazy dogs and cats would make mistakes and leave black paw prints on sidewalks and porches. Then they would sit and bite and whine at their strange black feet.

"How you getting over here?" yelled a voice. I looked up. Curly was standing at the corner of the church property with a lunch sack in his hand.

"Can't," I said forlornly. "Ma wouldn't let me for sure. She doesn't like oily shoes."

"Take your shoes off."

"And get my socks black?"

"Take your socks off."

"And get my feet black?"

"Then what *are* you going to do!"

"Can't come, I guess."

"Heck!" said Curly. "That means I gotta go with

Uncle Father to visit Mrs. Rakowski. She thinks she's dying again. She died three times last month."

"How could she die three times and again today?"

"She just thinks it. Uncle Father says she'll live to be a hundred."

That's why I like Curly. He knows all about dying and borning and marrying and church stuff. He says that Holy Water comes out of a regular faucet just like the water you brush your teeth in.

After Curly left I sat down in the ditch. The weeds tickled my chin while I thought. I sure wanted to eat my birthday lunch in the orchard. Even if I had to eat it alone. There had to be some way to cross Apple Road. That is to say, without getting oil on me. If I were Moses, the oil would spread apart, making a dry path for me to walk on. But I wasn't Moses. I was only Ignatius Zaska, who had never been to school. Maybe I could ride my bicycle. No, Ta wouldn't like oil on the tires. And Ma would say, "Oh, the beautiful bicycle ruined! And it costing five dollars secondhand yet!"

Maybe I could ride a big dog over. But I didn't know a big dog. Especially one that would let me sit on its back. Stilts? Could I make coffee-can stilts like those Reka made once? No, I'd have to ask Reka to help me, and she'd say, "You're too little, Ignatius. You'd fall for sure!"

I poked sadly at an old candy wrapper lying in the bottom of the ditch. Suddenly I had an idea. I knew how I could cross Apple Road safely without getting a speck of oil on me. I felt proud. I felt big. It was good to be five years old and smart already.

I ran to the back door and ducked down cellar.

There was the big stack of newspapers on the old chair, just as I remembered. I grabbed a bunch and ran outside. Carefully I did what I promised Ma I would do. I stopped, looked, and listened, even though I knew a car would never come splashing down Apple Road that day. Then I took a newspaper page from my bunch and lay it as far as I could onto Apple Road. I jumped onto it. It was like a beautiful square white island in a black sea. I stretched as far as I could and put down another page and jumped onto it. I was making stepping stones with newspapers. I had just enough to get all the way across the road to the orchard ditch. And there I was on the other side. Not a drop of oil on me.

But right away I knew someone in the orchard had been watching me.

4

I wasn't afraid though. I didn't know there was anything in the orchard to be afraid of— then. Trees were trees, and apples were apples. What was to be afraid? Suddenly two boys jumped out from a nearby tree cave.

"Hey, look who's here!" said the one with wild black hair falling over his eyes.

"I think we got us a new boy!" said the one with the red hair and the round sunburned face. "What's yer name?"

I stood up straight and proud. "My name is Ignatius Zaska, and my birthday is today."

"Ain't that some name!" remarked Black Hair. "And I'll bet yer about . . . Do you think he's ten years old, Willy?"

"At least ten. Maybe twenty," grinned red-faced Willy. I smiled uncertainly. I didn't know if they were teasing.

"I'm five," I said. "But I'm a big five, and I'll be going to school pretty soon."

"Big deal!" said Willy. "Ain't that a big deal, Jack!"

"Sure is," grinned Jack, and I saw something dance suddenly into his eyes. "Well, pleased to meet ya, kid. We'll be seeing ya around." And with that Jack punched Willy and they raced off between the trees.

I smiled. Two new friends already I had, and the orchard beckoned to me with twiggy fingers. Carefully I stowed my lunch in the tree cave where the boys had hidden. I saw the traces of a dirt path and started to follow it. The whole orchard began to sing and hum and strum as I walked into it. Later I knew it was the insects who sang the orchard songs all day and that the frogs joined in at night. But now, at the age of five, I thought the orchard sang. It was a calling song, and I followed it down the path, looking all around me.

I liked the path. I liked the path very much. I still like it. There's something about it that—that gives you goose bumps. The nice kind. Now, of course, I know that it is called Patch Path and that it meanders diagonally through the orchard and that it is the shortest way from my house to get to Pete's Friendly Store and The Pickly-Wickly Grocery over on Hannibal. The dirt of Patch Path is packed so hard you'd think a million feet had walked it. Sneakered feet. Booted feet. Bare feet. All kinds. And sled runners and wagon wheels, too. As the path lowers there are wide dirt steps made by tree roots.

I was only five, but already I loved Patch Path and I loved the orchard song and I loved something else, though at the time I couldn't put my mind to it. I guess it had something to do with getting away

from the peck-peck-peck and the cluck-cluck-cluck at home. Here there was no one to tell me my shirt was buttoned wrong or that one of my socks didn't match or that I was too little. Everything was perfect.

That is, until I came near the blackberry bushes. Then I heard a strange sound. I stopped to listen, but the sound stopped, too. When I started again, the sound started. With every step it happened. When I went fast, the sound went fast. When I went slow, the sound went slow. I wondered if I had a squeak in my shoes.

The path jig-jagged in the middle of the blackberry patch. I stopped suddenly in the jig of the jag. The sound didn't know I stopped, and it went on— oink . . . oink . . . oink—in its little voice. I wasn't afraid, I said to myself. After all, I was big now and had new friends in the orchard. Then why was my heart bumping around in my chest like a scared rabbit caught in a box? I listened carefully. The strange sound had stopped.

"I guess I'll go home now," I said aloud, as if talking to the sound. "I've got a cake at home for my birthday. It's a *baba* cake." I don't know why I talked out loud that way. I guess I needed to hear the sound of my own voice, even though it wasn't very big or very deep or very brave. I guess it helped though. It tamed the rabbit in my chest a little. I turned around and began to run up the path toward Apple Road. With the running of my feet came the sound again, this time not so mysterious. A voice was saying, "Oink . . . oink . . . oink . . . oink," with every step. And as I reached the road, it yelled, "Iggy, Iggy is a

31

Piggy. Iggy, Iggy is a Piggy! Iggy is a Piggy!"

So fast was I going I almost ran splitter-splatter, right onto black Apple Road. I skidded to a stop just in time. I hadn't been hurt in the orchard. I hadn't even been touched. Yet I knew I wanted to go home right away. I wanted to go home and look at the orchard from my own side of the road.

I looked for my newspaper stepping-stones. I was sure this was the very spot where I had laid them out. Not a paper was in sight. I could not even see where they had been. The black oil glistened and ran in little trickles in the sun. My house and the *baba* cake across the road seemed a million miles away.

"Hey, new kid," said a voice behind me. "What did you say yer name is again?"

I turned around and saw the big grins of Willy and Jack. I was glad to see them. They would help me.

"My name is Ignatius Zaska," I said.

"Oh, yeah!" said Jack. "Now, how could we forget a nice name like that, Willy?" He slapped Willy on the back and Willy snorted and coughed and turned redder than ever. I didn't know what to say.

"Something wrong, Ig?" asked Jack, coming closer, while Willy tumbled back in the weeds and rolled around in a very strange way. "Don't mind him. He's always having a fit!" Willy's fit seemed to get even fittier. I pulled my eyes away from something I didn't understand to something I did understand. I pointed to the road.

"My stepping stones are gone," I said. "I can't get back home."

"I do declare!" said Jack. "Ain't that a heck of a

problem though! It sure is funny, them stepping stones disappearing. Guess they blowed away."

"They couldn't blow. They were stuck in the oil," I said.

"Sure is a funny business. Well, we gotta be going, kid. Good luck!" The two boys thrashed off, and I was left looking at the river of oil through a river of tears. I had thought when I turned five I'd never cry again. I was getting too old to cry. That's what Ta had told me. Maybe it was the tarry smell making my eyes water.

I guess I know now that you're never too old to cry. That even grownups like Father Janowicz cry. But when you get older you learn how to hold it inside where it doesn't show.

I sat myself down in the weeds by the road. I guess I felt safer there because it was as close to home as I could get. I wondered about the missing stepping stones. Could a dog have taken them? A man from the City Department? A bird? It's funny that I never thought about a boy. It's funny that I never thought about two boys.

At least I knew one thing for sure. I'd have to find some other way to get back home. I could have stood there and yelled, "Ma! Felicia! Irka! Reka!" But I didn't. Being five years old seemed to make a big difference. I wondered, though, why my new big friends didn't help me. That's what friends were for, I thought.

The sun was straight overhead, drumming hunger on my head. Well, at least I still had my lunch. I went to the tree cave where I had hidden it. The sack was there. Only the sack. Did an animal eat my lunch? A small, hungry animal like a squirrel or a rabbit or even a tortoise? It's funny that I never thought about a boy. It's funny that I never thought about two boys. The mystery of the missing stepping stones and the missing lunch and the Iggy Piggy gave me a funny feeling.

I sure wished Curly was home. Maybe Curly could get me some jelly bread and help me think of a way to get back across the road. But he wasn't home, and Father Janowicz wasn't home. They were off helping Mrs. Rakowski die. Well, at least I could get a drink of water out of Father Janowicz's garden hose.

The idea came to me while I stood there with the water wetting my tongue and running down my chin, the warm rubbery-tasting water from the garden hose. I remembered that Father Janowicz saved newspapers like Ma. They were stacked in a shed where Father Janowicz kept his garden tools and his lawn mower and where he smoked his Christmas and Easter sausage. Maybe it would be all right to borrow some papers and pay Father Janowicz back from Ma's pile.

Into the dark hot shed I ran. The newspapers were gone! Every one! I wondered what Father had done with them. He was always giving things to the missionaries. Did he send them newspapers, too? I went back out into the hungry, thirsty sun and sat on Father's garbage can beside the shed. I wondered what missionaries did with a bunch of newspapers. I guessed they used some of them to wrap their garbage like everyone else. Garbage!

I jumped up as if the garbage can had been a hot seat. I pulled off the lid and found what I had hoped for—garbage. Garbage wrapped in newspapers. The top package was pretty dry. Carefully I unrolled it and let the eggshells and coffee grounds and prune pits drop back into the can. I guessed I knew what Curly and Father had had for breakfast.

There were just two pages, but already I had grown smarter. I knew I could get back across Apple Road with only two pages. I put the first page down in the oil and stepped on it. Then I put the second page in front of me as far as I could reach and stepped on it. Then I reached back and got the first page and moved it in front of me.

Soon I was back in my own safe yard. I bunched up the two oily papers and started toward the back of the house to put them in the trash. But I couldn't help turning around and looking over at the orchard. It was still singing its calling song, and its million twiggy fingers still said, "Come, come, come." Goose bumps there were on my arms. I couldn't tell whether they were the nice kind or the scary kind. Strange things had happened in the orchard. Very strange things. But already I knew I wanted to go back. Yes, I wanted to go back.

No one knew I had been in the orchard. Why didn't I tell? Ma and Felicia and Irka and Reka felt sorry for the bad luck of the oiled road on my birthday. Reka said, "Your picnic plans all ruined! Too bad, Ignatius!"

Irka said, "Well, there's one good thing. The orchard won't walk away! You can eat your lunch there another time, Ignatius."

Felicia said, "Don't cry, Ignatius," even though I wasn't crying.

And Ma hauled me up on her lap and said, "You're a big boy now. Big boys can wait." And she rocked me for awhile like I was a little boy. And there I rocked in Ma's lap with the orchard inside me like a big heavy lump. But still I didn't tell.

For four days the sun baked Apple Road into a hard black crust. Only the edges were sticky now. Car drivers were careful to stay in the middle so the loose black gravel at the edges would not fly up and stick to fenders and bumpers. One day Ma came with me and looked at the road. "Yes," she said. "I think you can go this time. You jump, Ignatius. You jump big over this sticky part. I'll fix you a lunch to take."

At last Curly and I could eat our lunch in the orchard. At last I could tell Curly my adventure and show him Patch Path and the blackberry bushes and . . . Hey, I had an idea!

"What's the bucket for?" asked Curly, as he watched me jumping carefully over the sticky parts of Apple Road.

"Something," I said importantly, leading the way to the nearest tree cave.

"But what?" asked Curly, hopping around me like a grasshopper.

"Tell you after we eat," I said shortly. I opened my lunch sack and took a bite of my peanut butter sandwich. Why didn't I tell my best friend Curly my great idea? Why didn't I tell him all of the exciting things that had happened on my birthday? My tongue wanted to get loose from the peanut butter and tell him. But I just sat and chewed. Something inside me wouldn't let me talk. Something told me to act like Mr. Big because I knew things Curly didn't know.

Two things already the orchard had made me do. Keep a secret from Ma and Felicia and Reka and

Irka. And play Mr. Big with my best friend, Curly. What else would the orchard teach me?

Ma had put the last piece of *baba* cake in my lunch. I looked at it a long time. Then I gave it to Curly, whose Uncle Father doesn't know how to make a *baba* cake. I guess it was the good part of me trying to make up for Mr. Big. Or maybe Mr. Big was just too full to eat it.

"Gee, thanks," said Curly, giving me a pickle in exchange. "Come on, Ignatius! Tell me now what the bucket's for."

"You don't need to call me Ignatius anymore," I said. "My friends in the orchard call me Ig."

"What friends?" asked Curly, frowning in wonder. And then I told him. All about the stepping-stones. All about my new friends, Jack and Willy. All about the missing lunch. All about Father Janowicz's garbage can. But not about "Iggy, Iggy is a Piggy." Mr. Big wouldn't let me tell him that.

"Wow!" said Curly, when I finished.

"This bucket's for blackberries," I continued. "Down that path there's a million blackberries! We can pick them and sell them and make a million dollars!"

"Wow!" said Curly.

"And I'm going to buy me—I'm going to buy me something BIG, real BIG! What'll you get?"

Curly thought for a long time. "I'd like some licorice from the Pickly-Wickly. And I guess I'll buy Uncle Father his window."

"What window?"

"The God window."

"What's a God window?"

"It's a window that has all the colors of the rainbow in it. But Uncle Father doesn't need a God window. He has a good plain window above the High Altar. You know. That round one. Instead, he needs paint and shingles and new soles for his shoes and a school coat for me. But still, he would like a God window."

"Does he pray for it?"

"Nope. He says you shouldn't pray for what you don't need. He says if God wants him to have a window with all the colors of the rainbow in it, it will happen."

"And it could happen, Curly!" I exclaimed. "We'll buy Father a God window together!"

"Wow!" said Curly. "Let's go!"

I grabbed the bucket and led the way down Patch Path. I ran and Curly was right behind me. I didn't hear any oink . . . oink . . . oink . . . oink. I was glad. But suddenly Curly said, "Wait! What's that over there?" One of the apple trees at the edge of the blackberry patch had something white fastened on it. We walked over.

"It's a note," said Curly.

"Yeah," I said and wished with all my heart I was six instead of five and knew how to read.

Just then a voice behind us said, "Well, look who's here again! It's old Ig! And he brought a friend!"

We turned around and there stood Jack and Willy and two other boys.

"What's yer friend's name, Ig?" asked Jack.

"It's Curly. He lives with Father Janowicz up by the church."

"He must be an awful good kid, to live by a church

that way," said Jack. "We sure are glad to get some new good kids in the orchard, ain't we guys!" Willy started snickering and getting red in the face, and the other boys just grinned.

"Now, what can we help you with?" asked Jack.

"It's this note," said Curly. "What does it say?"

"Hmm," said Jack, looking at the note. "This note don't belong on the Post Office Tree! This note don't even tell the truth! Hey, Bean, did you put this note up here?" Bean grinned and slowly shook his head.

"Did you, Chunk?"

"Nope," said Chunk, the short, fat boy.

"Willy, you wouldn't do a thing like that, would you?" said Jack. Willy snickered and covered his mouth quick.

"Willy has fits," I whispered to Curly, and we watched Willy's ears turn red and he went over and hid behind a tree.

"He didn't do it," said Jack. "Willy'd never do a thing like that."

"But what does the note say?" I asked.

"It says," said Jack, "BEWARE OF BEARS IN THE BLACKBERRIES." Curly and I stared at each other. Bears in the blackberries! "But it ain't true," went on Jack. "I ain't never seen no bear in the blackberries. I see you gotta bucket. If yer going ta pick berries, you go right ahead."

I picked up the bucket. "Of course," Jack said, "them blackberry brambles are mighty mean. You'll get scratched up for sure. Too bad you ain't dressed like bears. Bears don't feel even an eensy-weensy scratch through all that fur. You had oughta have bearskins to wear like them."

"I gotta couple-a bearskins they can wear," said Chunk. We could hear Willy having another fit behind the tree. Poor Willy. "Gimme yer shirts and I'll get em for ya," said Chunk. Curly and I looked at each other.

"Well, ya gotta take off yer shirts!" said Jack. "You'd be too hot wearing bearskins *and* shirts! A bearskin's mighty hot as it is. And yer lucky Chunk here's got a couple to lend ya." Slowly we unbuttoned our shirts and handed them to Chunk. He grabbed them and raced off like the wind. Jack and Willy whooped and hollered. Bean grinned from ear to ear.

"Well, there ya are," said Jack. "Yer standing in yer bare skins!" Then they all raced off in the direction Chunk had disappeared.

I remember how Curly and I stood and stared at each other's bare skins. I remember putting my hands on my own bare skin—just to see if it was really bare, I guess. It was bare, all right, and skinny. I could feel my ribs. A five-year-old chest isn't very broad or very tough.

"Some friends!" said Curly.

"Yeah, some friends!"

"What'll we do?"

"Well, we still have the bucket. Maybe if we pick the million berries and get the million dollars, Ta and your uncle will forget about our shirts being stolen."

"But the brambles will scratch us."

"We'll just have to be brave."

"Think there's a bear?"

"Naw. They were just trying to scare us!"

Plink. Plunk. Plonk. The berries zinged into the bucket. The bees zinged around our ears. The thorns zinged against our bare skins. The sun zinged hot on our heads. We picked and picked and picked. And when we'd picked about a million years, we looked into the bucket. The bottom was barely covered.

"We can't do it," said Curly. "We can't ever pick enough for a God window. And I itch! Come on, Ig. Let's go home."

I followed Curly forlornly up Patch Path. I sure didn't feel like Mr. Big anymore. I sure felt like mr. little.

"Hey, Ig! Look!" yelled Curly suddenly. There were our shirts hanging on the Post Office Tree. We put them on and buttoned them.

"Are you going to tell, Ig? About losing our shirts?"

I thought for a minute. "I don't know."

"Wanta divide the berries, Ig?"

"Naw. You and Father Janowicz can have them."

"Are you ever coming back here, Ig?"

This time I thought for a long time. Finally I nodded. "Yeah, I'm coming back." I crossed Apple Road and went home.

That night Ta was working in the cellar after supper.

"What are you doing, Ta?"

"You mean my son Ignatius cannot use his eyes?" Ta was right. It was a silly question. I could use my eyes, and I knew what Ta was making—tomato stakes for Ma's garden. I guess I just needed a way to start talking.

"Curly and I went to the orchard today," I said. "So?"

"The big kids played a trick on us."

"Did Ignatius Zaska cry?"

"No, Ta!"

"Good. And is Ignatius Zaska going back?"

"I think I will, Ta."

"Good. Now help me carry these tomato stakes to the garden."

When you're five, you walk into tricks as easy as puddles on a rainy day. When you're five, you believe what people in the orchard tell you. Sometimes you want to cry, but you don't except when no one's looking.

Then you turn six and you know the orchard better. You've been all the way down Patch Path to where it crosses Pie Creek and comes out on Hannibal. The bigger boys yell at you, and sometimes you are brave enough to yell back. Not in a great big voice. In maybe a little voice. But just the same it is yelling. And you learn to run fast. Very fast for your age and size.

Every time you step into the orchard, you get goose bumps. Scary, delicious goose bumps. Dangers dangle like apples in summer and icicles in winter, and you reach up to pick them. You can't seem to help picking, and you can't stay away from the orchard even when it hurts you.

"You're six," said Ma one day after school. "Reka's not here. Irka's not here. Felicia's not here. Do you think you're big enough to go to the store?"

I nodded my head excitedly. To carry money in my pocket? To speak myself to Mr. Perrini at the Pickly-Wickly? To carry home the important brown grocery bag? Yes, I was big enough.

"I'll give you money for bread. You get bread with seeds on, yes? And there should be money left for a candy." Ma put the money in my shirt pocket and pinned it shut with a safety pin. "You come right home. Hear?"

"I will, Ma," I said. Oh, the joy of the money jingling in my pocket as I ran down Patch Path. Past the Post Office Tree. Through the blackberry patch. Quickly by the haunted tree called the Northern Spy. Finally to Pie Creek where I stopped to decide what to do.

There is this about Pie Creek. Sometimes it is only a trickle no bigger than a drippy faucet. Sometimes it bounces along like the bubbles in Ma's noodle water. Sometimes there is a board thrown across the water for a footbridge. Who puts it there I don't know. But the boards aren't there long. I think they end up in the hands of the Willow Gang and become part of the Willow Tree House.

If the water is bouncy and wide, you have to decide what to do. If you have a father and mother who don't give a hoot, you just wade in with your shoes and socks on. But if you have a ta who will say when you get home, "And you think shoes grow on the apple trees?" and if you have a ma who will say, "Like boards these shoes are, and to church he must wear them!" and if you have sisters who will cluck and peck, then you think awhile. You can take off your shoes and socks and wade across, trying to dry your feet on your jeans legs before cramming them back into your socks and shoes. Or you can take a good look at the size of the creek and jump it if you think you can.

On this particular day Pie Creek was bouncy and wide. But with money in my pocket and going to the store, I felt especially big and sure. So I jumped. Pretty lucky I was. Only my heel got caught in the mud, and I wiped it off with a bunch of leaves.

At the end of Patch Path I stood on the curb of Hannibal and watched the traffic. A blue car passed. A green car passed. A dirty red truck passed. Then I crossed to the Pickly-Wickly.

"Well, look who's here," said Mr. Perrini. "Where are Reka and Irka and Felicia? You mean not one of those lazy sisters of yours would come to the store today?"

I laughed politely. Mr. Perrini liked to make people laugh. It's funny how some people like to make people laugh and some people like to make people scared and mad.

"And what is Ignatius Zaska going to buy?" asked Mr. Perrini.

"Bread," I said, trying to see down past my chin to unpin my pocket. "The kind with seeds that Ma always gets, please."

"Ah, yes," said Mr. Perrini. "You wouldn't like about three miles of wieners, would you, or a cheese as big as your head? Got a big sale going today."

I shook my head, laughing. "Oh, no, sir, Mr. Perrini! But I am to buy a candy if there is enough money left." I put my money into his hand. Quickly he counted it over.

"You are a lucky boy," he said. "You have enough left to buy a licorice whip, five rootbeer barrels, three jawbreakers, a packet of hotsies, or a honey bar. Take your pick." I decided on the honey bar. It would be chewy and last me all the way home through the orchard.

I carried the sack with bread in it carefully, making sure I didn't squeeze it too hard. I wanted my first trip to the store to be a just right trip so Ma would send me again. When I had jumped safely over Pie Creek I unwrapped my candy. I decided to count how many chews in a honey bar. There were five sections. I bit off the first and began to chew slowly. There were twenty-seven chews in the first part. I bit off the second section and began to chew. When you are chewing and counting and being careful not to squeeze the bread, you are not looking around you for danger. Your legs are not ready to run you at top speed in any direction. You are just plodding along and chewing.

That's just what I was doing when Jack and Chunk and Bean stepped onto Patch Path in front of me. "Whatcha got in that there bag, Ig?" asked Jack. Jack didn't make sweet talk anymore about being friends and all that.

"Just bread for my ma," I said.

"Got any money left?" asked Jack.

"Spent it all on a honey bar," I said, popping the rest of it into my mouth. A spark of triumph flashed through me then. I had put one over on the big kids. I had popped the whole bar in my mouth, and now they couldn't take it away from me. Now there was nothing they could do. They'd just have to get out of the way and let me walk home with Ma's bread.

"What kinda bread?" asked Chunk.

"Just seedy bread," I said.

"Hey, Jack," said Chunk. "That just happens to be

my favorite kind of bread. Is that your favorite kind of bread?"

"Sure is," said Jack. "How about you, Bean?" Bean grinned and nodded his head. Before I knew what was happening, Chunk had grabbed the sack of bread out of my arms.

"I'm glad you're one of them goody-good boys, Ig," said Jack. "Cause I know you won't tattle. If your ma wants to know where's the bread, you say you lost it. Understand? You're just an old klunk-head and you dropped it in Pie Creek. Understand?"

Chunk had opened the bread and the three of them began stuffing hunks into their mouths. I stood there watching them. I guess I hoped they'd leave some for me to take home.

"What's the matter, Ig-Pig?" said Jack. "Scared to go home without your ma's bread? Boy, are you gonna git it! Bet your old man gives you a whipping in the cellar tonight!"

I started home then, walking at first like I didn't care and I wasn't afraid. When I couldn't see them anymore, I ran. I don't know why I ran. Because when I ran, it got me home awfully fast and I wasn't ready yet with my answers.

Ma was looking out the front door when I got there. The first thing she said was, "Where's the bread?"

Six I was. Only six. I didn't know too much about tattling and lying. But I was going to have to learn fast. If I tattled on Jack and Chunk and Bean, what terrible things would happen to me? But if I lied, Father Janowicz said it was a sin and that a sin could lead you straight to *Pieklo*, which was a very hot terrible place. So I didn't say anything. Yet.

Ta was resting in the living room before supper. Felicia came in from the kitchen with a spoon in her hand. Irka stopped putting the plates on the dining room table and turned to look at me. Reka came clattering down from upstairs.

"Where's the bread?" repeated Ma. "Did you lose the money?" I shook my head.

"He's just fooling us, Ma," smiled Felicia. "He hid the bread on the porch." I shook my head.

"Did you lose the bread, then?" asked Irka. I

thought for a long minute because Irka was so close to the truth. Then I shook my head no again.

"He ate the bread!" laughed Reka. "He ate a whole loaf of bread!"

Then Ta, who was sitting quietly and watching me from his big chair, said, "Come here, Ignatius." I stood in front of Ta. It was like all the clucking hens were out of the room and only Ta and I were there to talk.

"You didn't lose the money and you didn't lose the bread," said Ta. "Did you buy the bread?" I nodded my head hard. I was still afraid to open my mouth because I didn't know what I wanted it to say. I hoped with all my heart Ta would help it to say the right thing.

"Then the bread disappeared somewhere between the store and home," said Ta. "And you say you didn't lose it. Then it was stolen!" I nodded hard.

"Who stole it?" gasped Felicia.

"I'll bet it was that Jack Campanelli," said Irka.

"Or maybe that strange boy named Bean or that silly Willy or that other kid—that Chunk. Was it one of them, Ig?" asked Reka. I gulped and looked desperately at Ta.

"To know it was stolen is enough," said Ta. "Names we do not need. The important thing is that Ignatius did not lie and Ignatius did not tattle. A loaf of bread is not a million dollars. If something important, something serious ever happens in the orchard, Ignatius will tell us. But we can eat our supper without bread, and that is that."

We ate without bread, and supper didn't taste much different. But, when we bowed our heads for the Holy Grace, I sure did thank God for Ta. And I crossed myself very, very carefully—not fast and hungry as I usually did. And that night Ma came and kissed me goodnight. "Ignatius," she whispered. "You are a big boy. You will go to the store another day. You'll bring home the bread all right!"

As we got older, Curly and I got braver. That is the way with all boys, I guess. We not only yelled back at Jack and Willy and Chunk and Bean, we began to sneak and spy on them. We were seven years old by then. Big cheeses we thought we were. Daredevils we thought we were. We began to wander from the near-safety of Patch Path, where a quick getaway was possible. We began to sneak farther and farther into the dangers of the lower orchard. That was where Jack and the other boys so often disappeared on the run. Where did they run, we wondered.

Curly and I would scoot slowly and silently on our stomachs through the high weeds. Sometimes we had to smother a sudden sneeze when we bumped into a dandelion puff or some sneezeweed. Sometimes we wriggled in quiet agony while a grasshopper danced inside our shirts. Sometimes we lay fearfully still while a bumblebee explored our ears. We risked ants in our pants and rocks in our socks and ticks and chiggers and burrs. And all for one reason. To creep close enough to spy on our enemies.

At first we thought Jack and Willy and Chunk and Bean hid out in the Willow Tree. That they had built the Tree House and owned the rope ladder dangling from it. But we soon knew the truth. We would hide under Tree Cave Number One, which was the best tree cave in the orchard. Like an apple umbrella it was. We would watch by the hour what went on in the lower orchard. That is how we knew the truth. Jack and Willy and Chunk and Bean were not the Willow Gang at all. They were just punks. That's what we heard the real Willow Gang call them.

The Willow Gang boys were big, maybe twelve or thirteen years old. Jack and his bunch were probably about nine or ten. Curly and I were only seven. The Willow Gang sat up in the Tree House and planned tricks to play on Jack and Willy and Chunk and Bean. We could hear their low voices and their loud laughs, but we could never hear what they were saying. They had a spyglass they used. Every little while they looked around the orchard with it. We trembled under our apple umbrella for fear we'd be seen.

After more stomach-scooting and itching and scratching and getting wet and muddy in the creek, we found out where Jack and Willy and Chunk and Bean hid out. It was at the corner of Apple and Pie Creek, where the creek runs through a big culvert under Apple Road. They had a pile of rocks outside their culvert. That way they could build a barricade or throw the rocks if they had to. We knew what they were doing in that culvert. Thinking up ways to fool Curly and me and get mean with us and act Mr. Big with us.

One day, as we crouched in Tree Cave Number One, watching, watching, I began to see the whole orchard for what it was. I whispered to Curly, "Those big kids, the Willow Gang, won't be the Willow Gang forever."

"Why not?" asked Curly, who wasn't thinking about much of anything just then.

"Because they'll grow up and do other things."

"Like what?"

"They'll be practicing basketball and football out at the high school and getting jobs."

"Hey, yeah!"

"And when they don't come around so much anymore, there will be a new Willow Tree Gang."

"Who?"

"Aw, come on, Curly. Use your brain. It'll be Jack and Willy and Chunk and Bean, of course."

"Hey, yeah!"

"And then we'll get the culvert. And someday you and I will get the Willow Tree. We'll be the Willow Tree Gang! You and me, Curly! Think of that!" I got so excited I almost forgot to whisper.

"I wonder how you get to be in the Gang. Do you have to fight one of them and win? Do you have to pay money?" said Curly.

"I don't know. But I guess you have to keep proving you're a tough cookie. That you're not a scaredy cat and that you can give as much as you take."

"We sure take a lot," said Curly. "But I can't think of any giving we do. Jack would tear us apart if we tried anything on him!"

"Yeah," I agreed. "It's easy for them. It's easy to be tough cookies when you're picking on kids littler and younger."

Maybe that was when the idea came to me. If it did, I didn't even know it until the day when Curly and I saw Marylou Polanski in the orchard by herself.

I don't know why Marylou was in the orchard. Mostly girls didn't come here. They played tea party and jacks on their front porches and roller-skated and hopscotched on the sidewalks. When Curly and I saw Marylou, she was sitting on a blanket under the Northern Spy tree cutting out paper dolls. Curly and I hid behind some blackberry bushes and watched her for awhile.

"Let's scare her," I whispered to Curly.

"How?"

"We could tell her the Northern Spy tree is haunted. We could tell her that a Northern spy is buried right where she's sitting. That ought to scare her!"

"But a Northern Spy is just a kind of apple, like a Grime's Golden or a Winesap. Uncle Father told us all about apples."

"But she doesn't know that. Let's scare her!"

"Yeah, let's." We split around the blackberry bushes on the run and skidded to a stop right in front of Marylou.

"Hey, kid," I said. "What you doing here?"

"What are you calling me kid for?" said Marylou. "You've known me for a million years, Ignatius."

"We're calling you kid because you don't belong here," said Curly.

"I have just as much right in this orchard as you do, Curly," said Marylou.

"But you're sitting under a haunted tree," I said.

"Haunted!" said Marylou. "Honestly—"

"That tree happens to be a Northern Spy tree," said Curly.

"Yeah," I said. "And maybe he's buried right where you're sitting!"

"Hah!" said Marylou and went right on cutting out paper dolls. Curly and I looked at each other. It sure wasn't easy being a tough cookie in the orchard. How could you be a tough cookie if you couldn't even scare anyone, not even a girl? And if you weren't a tough cookie, how could you ever be in the Willow Gang? I felt a pinch of worry. Was I going to be a little vanilla wafer forever?

That's when I tried to think what Jack would do. "Okay!" I said in a loud, mean voice. "If you like this haunted tree so much, you can stay here! We'll tie you to it!"

"You don't even have a rope," Marylou said. That was right. We didn't even have a rope. And then I remembered her braids. Marylou had sat right in front of me in church the Sunday before. I remembered thinking how her hair was like two old ropes hanging down over the back of the pew.

"Hold her, Curly!" I yelled. Marylou scrambled up in a hurry then. But Curly caught her and pinned down her arms. I grabbed her braids and managed

to tie them good and tight to a branch of the Northern Spy.

"So long, kid," I snarled, like Jack would have done.

"So long, kid," said Curly, and a little giggle flipped out of his mouth. I hoped he wasn't going to have a giggle fit like Willy. Slow and cool we walked to the blackberry bushes and then sat down to watch her where she couldn't see us. I waited for the feeling to come over me like I'd seen in the eyes of the other boys. I guess Curly was waiting for that same feeling—that wonderful, tough, ha-ha-ha feeling. It sure was a neat trick we'd pulled. Marylou couldn't even sit down. She had to stand there with her paper dolls scattered all around her feet.

Just then we heard Father Janowicz whistle. "Gotta go," whispered Curly. "See ya." And he dashed off for the church property. That left me all alone with our first tough cookie of a trick. I didn't exactly like being all alone.

Marylou was standing there with her arms up trying to get her hair unsnarled. I decided I was glad it was Marylou and not some other little kid I didn't know. Marylou had stuck her tongue out at me during church Sunday. It was during Father Janowicz's sermon when I was looking at her long hair ropes. I guess Father Janowicz's sermons are worth listening to if you understand Polish good. At least the mothers and fathers and grandparents seem to listen. Though sometimes their eyes are closed, and you can't tell. But us kids, who know about every fifth word in Polish, can't even get the story of Noah straight. So when the standings and sittings and kneelings and prayings are over and everyone settles down for the sermon, I guess the kids all think about other things. At least I do. That was when, last Sunday, Marylou turned smack around and stuck her tongue out at me. And I didn't even touch her old rope braids.

After church I heard Irka say to Felicia, "That Marylou Polanski is a cheeky little thing. She stuck her tongue out at Ignatius." I didn't know why Irka called her cheeky. I didn't know what it meant. I'd have called her tonguey. But it made me feel better to know that Marylou was a cheeky little thing. She probably deserved what she was getting now.

She struggled for awhile longer, and then I guess her arms got tired. I wondered why she didn't yell for help. But she didn't. She just started to cry. A quiet little cry. I guess that's when I knew the wonderful, tough, ha-ha-ha feeling was never going to come. I guess that's when I knew I'd never feel like a tough cookie doing stuff like this.

She cried louder, and I put my hands to my ears. I wondered if all the apple trees were putting their hands to their ears. I don't think the orchard was used to hearing crying. If a kid had to cry, he did it inside himself where it didn't show. That was sort of the law of the orchard. Of course, the orchard wasn't used to girls.

Well, girls I knew all about. I had three big ones at home without counting Ma. And I knew that you could put your hands up to your ears just so long and then you had to do something about their bawling and sniffling and carrying on. You had to do something about it even when it was the fault of some dumb boyfriend or a grouchy schoolteacher or a broken string of beads. So you gave them a flower, even if it was just a dandelion. Or you brought them a glass of water, even if they weren't thirsty. Or you gave them one of your lucky marbles. And pretty soon everything was all right.

Well, I couldn't stand Marylou's crying anymore. I walked slowly around the blackberry bushes. Marylou's eyes were all puffy, and her face was streaked with dirt and tears. She didn't say anything. Just watched me coming. "I'm sorry, Marylou," I said, and I got busy working on her snarled hair. Boy, she'd made a mess of it trying to get it untied and not being able to see what she was doing. I worked and worked. "It's no use," I finally said. "I can't untie it." I thought she'd really bawl when I said that. But she didn't.

"Cut it off then," she said and pointed to her paper-doll scissors on the blanket. Cut it off! Why, Ma and Felicia and Irka and Reka had never cut their hair! Their hair reached past their waists when they let it down. On hair-washing day at our house, we had hair all over the place. Ta always stayed away. He said it was like living in a hair factory.

"Cut it off, Ignatius," Marylou said again. "I'm getting awful tired of standing here." So that's what I did. The paper-doll scissors weren't very sharp and it took a lot of cutting, but I did it. I cut one braid, and there stood Marylou with her other braid hanging down, and attached to it was the one I'd cut loose from her head. She looked awful. I helped her pick up her paperdolls and fold up her blanket, and away she walked out of the orchard without another word.

I didn't know what to do. I just wandered up Patch Path in a sort of daze and went home. I lay on my bed all afternoon and tried to think what to do. Ta had said that I was a boy who didn't tattle and didn't lie. But he said that if ever something important, something serious happened in the orchard I would tell. What I didn't know was how important, how serious was tying Marylou to a tree and cutting off her braid. Should I tell?

I decided to wait. Maybe I would find out how important it was by waiting. Maybe the telephone would ring, and I would find out for sure how important it was. Ma came to my room and thought I was sick. She felt my head to see if it was hot. She felt my feet to see if they were cold. She felt my stomach to see if it hurt. But she forgot about my heart. I guess my heart was what was sick. Sick about lopsided Marylou Polanski.

Ma brought me a cup of chicken broth for supper. I drank it and listened for the telephone. It didn't ring. Felicia read to me a story about a fish and Irka read to me a story about a magic umbrella and Reka read to me about Noah and the Ark. I didn't hear any of the stories because I was too busy listening for the telephone. It didn't ring.

Ta looked in the bedroom door. "You do not have a fever, Ignatius? No chill? Your stomach does not hurt? What kind of a sickness do you have?"

"I don't know exactly, Ta. Pills won't help it though," I said.

"Oh, it's that kind," said Ta. "Well, you know where to find me if you need me. Good night."

And the telephone didn't ring.

9

When I came down the stairs the next morning and saw Ma setting out the breakfast in her black silk dress, I remembered it was Sunday. Ma hurried over to me. "Oh, Ignatius! Maybe you shouldn't go to church. You feel bad, yes?"

I was feeling bad, all right. Like I hadn't slept all night. But Ta was sitting on the kitchen stepstool sipping coffee. He answered for me. "Ignatius will go to church. He will eat his bowl of cornflakes and go to church."

So I went to church. We all walked across Apple Road together, and I tried to lose myself in the middle of the silky, swishy dresses of my sisters. "Walk ahead, Ignatius," said Felicia. "You're going to trip us."

I was probably the most devout boy who ever stepped inside the Polish-in-America Church. I dipped my fingers most tenderly into the Holy Water. I made the Sign of the Cross as if I had a ruler to measure by. I bowed so deeply to the High Altar, I almost lost my balance and fell down. I sank to the kneeling bench and prayed and prayed and prayed—longer than anyone else in my row. All I could think of to pray was, "Please, please, please." I don't know what I meant by "Please." But I guess God thought I meant please let me sit right behind Marylou Polanski. Because when I got up from my knees and sat down on the pew, there she was. Her hair was short all over in ringlets. I saw Curly across the aisle, and he raised his eyebrows at me. Lucky Curly. To have been called by his Uncle Father's whistle. Curly didn't even know why Marylou's hair was so short. I wondered how many people did know why Marylou's hair was so short.

I guess that was the longest church service I ever sat through. Marylou didn't turn around once to stick out her tongue. When Father Janowicz finally said the last Amen, I was the first one out of there.

And right behind me was Marylou. She followed me around to the back of the church. "Wait, Ig, wait!" she called.

Beside a lilac bush I stopped where folks couldn't see us much. We stood there looking at each other and breathing hard. "I just wanted to say thanks," she said.

I, Ignatius Zaska, couldn't believe my ears! Marylou went on. "I wanted to cut my hair for ages and ages, but Mama wouldn't let me. I didn't tell on you, honest, Ig. I said I got my hair tangled in a tree branch and had to cut it to get loose." Marylou smiled and danced around me. "Look at it, Ig! Isn't it beautiful?"

It *was* kind of beautiful, and suddenly my heart felt better. I decided that if Marylou had been sad

or mad, I'd have had to tell Ta. But as long as she was happy, it wasn't important enough to tell. I reached out and pulled one of Marylou's corkscrew curls. Not hard. Just a little. Bwang! It bounced right back to her head! "Yeah," I said. "It's real neat, Marylou."

Curly and I turned eight, and we found a paper. If the paper had been nailed to the Post Office Tree, we'd have known right away it was a trick. Probably Jack's.

But the paper wasn't on the Post Office Tree. It was half-buried beside Patch Path where Patch Path jig-jags through the blackberry bushes. Right there in the jig of the jag—that's where the paper was.

Curly brushed off the dirt. Very old the paper looked. It was yellowish and had strange dark markings on it. Right away I felt the oldness of the orchard all around us. The crooked trees were like old men trying to see over our shoulders. They probably knew something about this paper—how old it was, who had left it, what it meant.

"Maybe it's a pirate map," said Curly.

"But we're a million miles from the ocean," I said. We carried it to a sunny corner of the orchard up near the church property and spread it out on the ground. That was when I thought I heard a branch snap. "Hide it!" I whispered to Curly and he, quick, stuffed it in his shirt.

Now, what did that mean—the snapping of a branch? We looked all around us. No one was in sight. Curly pulled the paper out again. Like a map it didn't look. That was for sure. There were no South,

East, North, West on it. No words said: Walk ten paces to the mossy rock, face the sun, walk until your feet are wet, turn left, look for the eagle's nest. It was just an old-looking paper with X's on it and one arrow and one word. And what a dumb word— pib.

"What does pib mean?" I asked Curly.

"Never heard of it."

"Is it Polish?"

"Ig, you know I can't read Polish," said Curly. "But we could ask Uncle Father."

"Naw," I said. Somehow, sharing the strange, old paper with a grown-up would spoil it. "Why can't we look it up ourselves? We can use Father's English dictionary and his Polish dictionary. Will he let us?"

"Sure," said Curly. We dashed to the manse with the paper carefully stuffed inside Curly's shirt. Father wasn't there. "I think he's at the church," said Curly.

Father was trimming wax from the candles and taking short ones out and putting tall ones in. We waited quietly beside him. The sun shone in the plain round window above the High Altar and made a spotlight on Father. I blinked my eyes in the brightness. If that was a God window up there with all the colors of the rainbow in it, Father would be standing in violet or yellow or red or blue or a whole bunch of colors mixed together. I wondered if Father was thinking about that as he carefully trimmed the candles with his pocketknife. He must have been thinking about something deep, maybe even praying, because he certainly wasn't thinking about us. On one leg I stood and then on the other. Curly rolled his eyes at me.

Finally Father looked up. "Ah, boys," he said.

"Can we—may we use your dictionaries, Uncle Father?" asked Curly.

"Oi, you want education in the summer yet?" said Father. "Yah, I like that. You use dictionaries in the summer. You get smart."

"Thank you, Uncle Father," said Curly.

"Thank you, Father," I said. We walked sedately out of the church and split for the manse and Father's study.

"Let's use the English dictionary first," I said. Carefully we turned the thin pages. "Pia——, pib——, hmm. The closest thing is pibroch."

"What does it mean?" asked Curly.

"'A kind of musical piece performed on the bagpipe.' That couldn't be right."

"Maybe all the strange X's on the paper are music for the bagpipe."

"Naw. That's silly. Let's look in the Polish dictionary." I opened up the big Polish dictionary and began to turn the pages. "Pia——, pic——. Hey! It jumps from *piatek* to *picie*. There isn't even a word starting with pib!"

"Well, it's a good thing," said Curly.

"Why?"

"We can't read Polish anyhow."

Curly was right. It's funny how a language you don't know looks like chicken tracks. It's funny how Ma and Ta and Father Janowicz can take those Polish chicken tracks and turn them into real everyday words.

We wandered back outdoors. I kept thinking about the bagpipe music but couldn't make any sense out of it. Once more we spread our paper out on the ground. The X's were all in neat rows. The arrow pointed to one of the X's. And then there was that strange word ριⷨ .

"It isn't very clear," said Curly. "Maybe the word isn't pib. Maybe it's pig." I thought about that for awhile. If this paper said pig, then it had something to do with Jack and Iggy, Iggy is a Piggy. I turned the paper over to look on the back.

"Hey, Curly!" I yelled. "We've been looking at the wrong side. We've been looking through the paper and everything was backwards. This side is much clearer and the word isn't ριⷨ . It's ⷣιϥ !"

Now that made sense. A map it had to be then. A treasure map, maybe. But what were the X's? That's when we thought we heard a dry rustle and a squeak. Some bird noise it could have been. The orchard was full of birds. But we couldn't be sure. Quickly Curly stuffed the map inside his shirt again. "I think someone's spying," he whispered.

"Maybe it's Jack. Maybe this map is one of his tricks," I said.

"But it looks so old!" exclaimed Curly. "It even feels old!"

"Yeah," I agreed. "Let's take another look." There were the X's all over the map. Five rows of them there were. I closed my eyes to think. The minute I closed my eyes I remembered visiting the bell tower of the church one day with Curly. It was cold up there because it was winter. I remembered looking down on the orchard and thinking how strange the bare black branches of the trees looked against the snow. Like black X's on a white paper.

"It's a map of the orchard," I breathed in wonder. "The X's are the trees."

"Come on!" urged Curly. "All we have to do now is count off the trees till we find the one with the arrow and start digging!"

"Nope," I said.

"Oh," said Curly. "You mean we ought to get shovels first?"

"Nope," I said. "If this is a trick, Curly, sure as shooting we're being watched. Sure as shooting they'll follow us to the tree on the map. Sure as shooting we'll dig and dig and dig and they'll laugh and laugh and laugh because there won't be anything there."

"Hey, yeah," said Curly. "But what if it's for real, Ig?"

"I don't know. All I know is that I don't want to be tricked again!"

"Well, what'll we do?"

I thought and thought. Some way there had to be to play it safe. Some way to turn the trick on Jack and his bunch, if it was a trick. We were eight years old going on nine. We had spent too many years in the orchard getting laughed at. If I had to stay up all night, I decided, I'd think of a way to turn the laugh on Jack and Willy and Chunk and Bean.

"Meet me here tomorrow, Curly," I said. "Bring the map and a shovel."

It took some doing. I had to make a telephone call to a boy I knew from school. Eight blocks I had to bike to that boy's house and borrow something. But the next morning I was ready, with Ta's shovel in my hand and something in my pocket. Curly was waiting with another shovel and the map.

X X X X X X X X
X X X X X X X X
X X dig→X X X X X
X X X X X X X
X X X X X X X

We looked at the map again. Then we started counting off the orchard trees. We walked quietly and did our counting in whispers. The tree we came to looked pretty ordinary. It was awfully close to the Old Willow, but the Willow Gang was nowhere in sight. In fact, there seemed to be not another living creature in the orchard except for birds and bugs and maybe some rabbits and squirrels. Yet I felt we were being watched. We hadn't heard anyone following us, but they could have already been staked out in hiding places close by. Well, it didn't matter to me. I patted my pocket.

"Which side should we dig on?" whispered Curly. We checked the map again and decided to dig at the point of the arrow. The ground was pretty soft because we'd had a humdinger of a rain two days ago. But there were lots of tree roots in the way. We dug and dug. It was hot work.

"I wonder what someone could have buried here," said Curly.

"Maybe some money during the War Between the States."

"Yeah. Or maybe Mister Meister's wife's jewels."

"Maybe someone robbed a bank and hid the loot here!"

"It might even be a skeleton. Boy, would that be neat!" said Curly.

By this time the hole was big enough for one of us to get into. We took turns in there loosening the dirt and tossing it up. We were really sweating and getting awful tired when it happened. It seemed suddenly that the whole orchard was full of whoops and hollers. I was the one down in the hole then. The minute I heard those whoops and hollers I quickly dropped what I had in my pocket and stamped it into the dirt. In no time at all Jack and Willy and Chunk and Bean were standing around the hole.

"Well, if it ain't old Ig-Pig and Girly-Curly," said Jack. "Whatcha doing, fellas?"

"Digging," said Curly. "Use your eyes!"

"Whatcha digging for?" asked Chunk.

I leaned on my shovel. "Well, we found this old, old map, didn't we Curly? We think it might be a map of the orchard and that maybe something's buried here." When I said that, Willy began to snort behind his hand and Jack kicked him.

"Gee whiz!" said Jack. "Let's see the old, old map."

"Well, I don't know," I said. "Promise you'll handle it pretty careful. And I'm telling you right now, whatever we find here belongs to Curly and me!"

"Sure, man," said Jack. "Just let us take a peek at that old, old map."

Curly took it out of his shirt and handed it to Jack. "Hey," said Jack, "this map looks kinda familiar. Have you seen this map before, Chunk?" Chunk shook his head.

"Have you seen this map before, Willy?" Willy began to giggle.

"Have you seen this map before, Bean?"

"Yeah," grinned Bean in his slow way. "You made it, Jack."

"I don't believe it," said Curly. "This map is too old. It even feels old."

"Wanta know how old it is?" said Jack. "I made it and put it beside Patch Path night before last. Anything that's out that long looks old!"

"I still don't believe it," I said. "I'm going to keep digging." I shoveled out a couple more loads of dirt. "Hey!" I said, acting excited. "I think I hit something!" I got down on my knees and felt around in the dirt at my feet. "Well, look at that! Curly, we did it! We found the treasure!" I handed my find up to Curly.

"Wow!" said Curly. "Real Indian arrowheads! Two of them! One for you and one for me!"

"Come on!" I yelled. "Let's go show them to Father Janowicz!" We grabbed our shovels and got the heck out of there. We'd learned not to wait around. Waiting around ten seconds too long in the orchard could mean losing whatever you had.

Jack and Willy and Chunk and Bean didn't follow us though. We looked back and they were on their hands and knees around the hole. Curly wasn't even disappointed when I told him where the arrowheads had come from and that we had to give them back.

All the next week we saw Jack and Willy and Chunk and Bean hunting around and digging around for arrowheads. Every time we saw them we laughed inside ourselves. I guess it was the wonderful, tough, ha-ha-ha feeling we'd been hunting for a long time. And we didn't have to make girls or little kids cry to get it either.

After that Jack and his bunch let us alone for awhile. I guess they were thinking twice about Curly and me. We even got kind of friendly. But it didn't last long.

It was the caterpillar time of the year. Everywhere you looked you'd see one inching along. All

kinds there were. Long thin ones. Short fat ones.
Naked rubbery ones. Hairy ones. Some with spines
and some with horns.

Curly and I decided we'd catch a couple for pets and
maybe watch them make cocoons. Father Janowicz
told us the best way to catch them. He said to see
what kind of leaves they were feeding on. Then put
the caterpillars and some of those leaves in a jar with
holes in the lid. He said to keep feeding them the
same kinds of leaves because that's the kind they
liked the best.

I decided on a big fat green one I found climbing
down a tree trunk on the church property. It looked
tough and brave. And yet it looked fat and jolly. I
decided to name it Jolly.

Curly liked the fuzzy-wuzzies the best. One day
we found one that rolled up into a ball when Curly
touched it. Father Janowicz said that it was called a
Woolly Bear, so that's what Curly named it.

Well, when Jack and Willy and Chunk and Bean
saw what we were doing, they decided to get them-
selves caterpillars, too. Bean caught himself an inchworm, which Father said was really a caterpillar
even though folks called it a worm. Bean would sit
by the hour letting his inchworm measure him all
over, like it was measuring him for a suit of clothes
or something.

Chunk found a beauty that was black and yellow
striped. He called it Tiger.

Willy found a caterpillar on a milkweed. It had
whiskers growing out both ends. It looked like it had
decided to grow a moustache or else was too poor to
go to the barber. Willy named it Mr. Whiskers.

Jack caught himself the biggest caterpillar of all. Almost five inches long, it was, with bright stripes and lots of horns on top. We looked it up in Father's book and found out it was a Hickory Horned Devil. Boy, old Jack was really pleased with himself. Of course, he named his Devil.

So there we were with our zoo of caterpillars. I guess it was really the first thing we six had ever done together without someone getting mad or sly. Of course, as it turned out, things got worse fast.

"Let's have a caterpillar race," said Jack. "We'll see whose caterpillar can crawl the fastest. We'll name the winner The Champeen Caterpillar of the Orchard."

"Hey, neat!" said Curly.

"But we have to lay down the rules first," I said. By this time I knew Jack pretty well. Unless rules were laid down first, he made them up as he went along and you know who always ended up winning. Jack seemed like a boy who had to win. I always wondered why. Maybe at home he was always a loser. Maybe in school he wasn't so hot either.

"Okay," said Jack. "First with a stick we draw a little circle in the dirt and put all the caterpillars in that little circle. Then we draw a big circle around the little circle. When we say Go, the first caterpillar to cross the big outside circle is the winner."

That sounded fair to me. "But you can't touch your caterpillar," I added. "And you can't step inside either circle once the race has started."

"But you can reach as far as you can with a juicy leaf and try to get your caterpillar to follow it," said Chunk.

"But if you fall into the circle or even step on the line, you're out of the race," I said.

Everybody nodded his head. The rules sounded fair enough.

"And I'll be the one to say Go," said Jack.

I knew Jack would have to be the big wheel somehow. Well, it didn't matter to me who said, "Go." I began to think about our caterpillars and what chances they had to win the race. Curly's Woolly Bear was cute, but I couldn't see that it had a chance in a million to win. It rolled up in a ball at the drop of a hat. I guess it was a scaredy cat. Jack and I both had big powerful bruisers. I thought they'd make a good match. Maybe they weren't the fastest, but they'd be strong and stick to it. I didn't know much about Willy's Mr. Whiskers or Chunk's Tiger, but I knew Bean had a speed demon. That little old inchworm could measure up a leg or down an arm in no time flat—if he was in the mood. Sometimes he just liked to hang onto a stick and look like a twig. Well, we'd soon find out if he felt like a twig or a speed demon today.

We began to hunt for a good place for the racing circle. Everywhere we looked in the orchard there were things growing and humped-up tree roots. What we needed was a big smooth place of just plain dirt.

"If we just had a bedsheet," said Jack, "we could spread it out most anywhere and make a humdinger of a track. Chunk, go get us a bedsheet."

Chunk squirted out of sight and in no time was back with a sheet and about a dozen little kids following him. I wondered how he talked his mother into giving him a sheet so fast. Ma would have needed a half hour of explaining and begging, with Felicia and Irka and Reka telling her why I shouldn't have it. And I wouldn't have gotten it, that's for sure. I didn't think too many mothers would lend their sheets for a caterpillar race.

I wasn't surprised at all to see the little kids, some of them not so little, some of them girls. More and more of them had been playing in the orchard lately. I guess it was because Curly and I left them alone and Jack and his bunch were too busy sidestepping the Willow Gang and handling Curly and me to bother with them. Exciting it was, them being there. The little kids, that is. It made the race seem like a big thing, with a cheering section and all.

"If we fold the sheet, we can find the middle," I said. Jack and I held up the sheet and carefully folded it twice. Then Jack stuck a burr where the center was and we spread the sheet on the ground. With a stick that Chunk had stabbed in the muddy creek bottom, Jack drew a small circle in the center of the sheet and then a larger circle around it.

"Okay. Stand back everybody," said Jack importantly. We got our caterpillars out of our jars and put them all in the center circle in the center of the sheet. Then we quick stepped back and Jack yelled, "GO!"

Well, I guess those caterpillars ddin't understand English. When Jack said, Go! they weren't in any hurry at all.

"Come on, Jolly!"

"Here, Whiskers! Here, boy!"

"Giddy-up, Tiger!"

"Faster, faster, you Devil!"

"Aw, get going, Woolly Bear!"

I guess the only kid who wasn't yelling was Bean. He didn't have to yell. His inchworm was busy as the dickens measuring that sheet. The trouble was, it kept measuring in circles instead of straight. The other caterpillars were just as dumb but slower. Willy's Mr. Whiskers seem to be the only one in the bunch with a sense of direction. In spite of his bushy whiskers, he seemed to be able to see where he was going. Finally he made it over the outside circle.

"Hooray! Hooray!" yelled all the little kids and girls. Willy's freckled face got red. I guess it was a happy red.

"Mr. Whiskers is The Champeen Caterpillar of the Orchard!" I yelled.

Jack frowned. "Two out of three!" he yelled. "Let's make it two wins out of three!"

"Those weren't the rules," I said.

"Okay, okay," he muttered. "But let's have another race anyhow."

So we all put our caterpillars in the center ring again. That's when Jack looked around at all of us and said, "Chicken?"

"What do you mean—chicken?" asked Curly.

"Let's step on them. Let's squash them all. Chicken if ya don't!" And Jack plunked his sneaker right down on top of his Hickory Horned Devil. You should have heard the little kids squeal. Then everybody was stamping around on that sheet—except me. I just stood there. Why would I want to step on poor Jolly? I liked Jolly. Someday I hoped to watch Jolly make a cocoon and turn into a beautiful moth. Of course, I could always catch another caterpillar. But heck! Jolly was Jolly! I looked at Willy and there he was with the others, killing his own Champeen. Even Curly was in there.

When the excitement finally settled down, Jack looked at me. "Chicken!" he snarled. "Ig's a chicken!"

I picked up my empty jar and started to leave. I knew I should yell something back at Jack, but I couldn't trust my voice. Just think. Me! A nine-year-old orchard kid with a throatful of tears on account of a crazy old caterpillar named Jolly.

"Hey, Ig!" yelled Chunk. "Don't forget your sheet!" I turned around and stared at Chunk. "Your house was the closest, Ig-Chicken, so I borrowed it off your ma's clothesline!"

Jack chortled. "Say thanks to your ma, Ig!"

Everybody scattered fast then except me and Curly and someone else. It was Marylou.

"Hey, Ig," said Marylou. I looked up surprised. I guess I hadn't even noticed that Marylou was at the caterpillar race. She held something out to me. It was a fat green caterpillar.

"I don't want another one," I said, shaking my head.

"But it's Jolly!" said Marylou. "I just reached in there and grabbed him! Almost got my fingers smashed, for goodness sakes! Take him!"

So I took Jolly and felt the familiar tickle of his feet on my hand. Marylou balled up the gruesome-looking bedsheet and handed it to me. "Good luck, Ig," she said. "You're going to need it!"

And do you know I couldn't even say thanks? What kind of a kid was I anyhow? I sure wasn't much of a tough cookie with all those tears boiling around inside me like Pie Creek after a spring rain.

"Ma!" yelled Felicia. "Here comes Ig with your lost sheet. I told you he'd find it for you!"

"My gosh, Ig!" said Irka. "Why did you ball it all up? It should be folded!"

"How did *you* get Ma's sheet, anyhow?" asked Reka, taking it out of my arms. "Gag! Ignatius Zaska! What did you do to Ma's sheet?"

"Did *you* do it, Ig?" said Felicia, holding her nose.

"Who did it?" asked Irka, backing away.

"I'll bet it was that Jack Campanelli," said Reka.

Ma came in the room then. She threw up her hands when she saw the sheet. "Take it to the cellar, Reka!" she said. Ma sat down weakly in a chair. She

looked and looked at me standing there with Jolly in his jar. Finally she said, "I ask and ask questions but no use. When you go to the orchard, your tongue never works!" For a minute I thought Ma was going to cry. She shrugged her shoulders then and started toward the kitchen. "We'll wait for your ta," she said. "We'll show him the sheet and he will decide."

When Ta got home from the rubber factory, all tired and dirty, his eyes studied the sheet and studied me a long, long while. He didn't ask how or who or why. I knew that he expected me to tell him anything important or serious that happened in the orchard. It was a hard thing to decide. I knew Ma's sheet was important to *her*. Should I tell Ta that Chunk had stolen the sheet off Ma's line? Should I tattle on Chunk? Heck, I didn't even like Chunk much. It shouldn't matter.

I was glad Ta spoke then because I didn't have to make up my mind. He said, "Ignatius, I give to you this sheet for a present. You will sleep on it every night until it wears out. You can sleep on it the way it is, or you can try to get it clean. It is nothing to me." Then Ta went slowly up the cellar stairs to go and wash off the rubber factory dirt and change his clothes.

I threw the sheet into a tub with hot water and a bunch of soap. I decided I'd let it soak overnight and get to work on it in the morning. It wouldn't be too bad sleeping on the bare mattress for one night. Maybe I could even fold over my other sheet and sleep in it like a sandwich.

It took me three days of washing and rubbing and bleaching and boiling. All the stains never did come out. Every single night I went to bed after that, the stained sheet reminded me of the caterpillar race. And every washday after that I had to look at my stained sheet hanging on the line and hear Ma say, "Oh, dear! What the neighbors must think!"

When I finally got back to the orchard three days later, there didn't seem to be anyone there. I knew Curly had to be around somewhere because I had asked Father Janowicz. I checked the whole upper orchard and carefully worked my way down toward the Old Willow and the culvert. No one was in the Willow. So I crawled silently toward the culvert. Maybe they had Curly in there as a prisoner! Behind a thick stand of cattails I stopped and listened. I could hear voices. I was sure one of them was Curly's. I was just wondering how I could rescue him, when he came walking out into the sunshine followed by Bean. They seemed to be alone, so I stood up.

"Hey, Ig!" yelled Curly. "Guess what! Jack and Willy and Chunk were init- initiated into the Willow Gang. Now we get the culvert!"

"But what about Bean?" Curly and I both turned to look at Bean. I guess we realized then that we didn't know Bean very well. He never talked much. Just did a lot of grinning. And his grin always spread across his face slow as molasses. Always he seemed to be last, loping behind the other boys. Always he seemed to be doing what someone else told him to do.

"Aren't you going to be in the Willow Gang?" I asked.

Bean shrugged his shoulders and grinned. "Guess not," he said. I didn't say any more. I decided he hadn't been invited. Funny that a good-natured, willing boy like Bean wouldn't be invited. I guess the Willow Gang didn't think he was tough enough. I couldn't tell whether Bean felt sad or not. But I felt a sudden urge to do something nice for him.

"Golly, Bean," I said, "we'd sure be proud if you'd join our gang. Wouldn't we, Curly?"

"Hey, yeah, Bean," said Curly. "We've always been shorthanded. Will you join us?"

Bean's grin started at the corners of his mouth and spread even to his ears. They did a little wiggle he was so happy.

So now we were three, like the Three Musketeers or the Three Stooges or the Three Little Pigs. We walked together up toward Patch Path. Bean was much the tallest. I wondered how old Bean was. Some day, if he ever got up some speed, he'd make a heck of a basketball player.

"What'll we do first?" asked Curly.

I kept thinking about getting up Bean's speed. "Why don't we have some footraces?" I said. "We could all use the practice."

"Hey, yeah," agreed Curly. "We can start up at the top of Patch Path and mark the end of the track just before we get to the blackberries. I'll run down and mark it, and you two get ready. Then I'll call 'Go.'"

Bean and I stood side by side at the top of the path waiting for Curly to yell "Go." Boy, if Bean poured himself into this race with those long legs of his, I knew I didn't have a chance. I'd really have to hustle. Off like a flash I was, the minute I heard Curly's signal. For three seconds, maybe, Bean and I pounded the dirt of Patch Path neck and neck. Then I quickly drew away and crossed the finish line far, far ahead of him. Wow! I never knew I was so fast!

"Let me try," said Curly, when he saw the outcome of the race. Curly and I had raced each other so many times, it wasn't any fun. We were so evenly matched that it seemed we just took turns winning and losing. But this was different. Here was a much bigger, older boy with longer legs. If we could beat him, we must really be something!

So I stayed down at the finish line, and this time Curly and Bean raced. Curly beat by a mile. I looked at Bean's face as he came loping in. He was grinning ear to ear. "You guys are good," he drawled.

"Are you running as fast as you can, Bean?"

"Sure am," he said. "You guys are good."

Race after race we ran, and we always beat him. We gave him bigger and bigger headstarts, but we always won. We won and won and won. Victory sang in our hearts and we wore wings. And Bean never got mad. He never asked to quit. He just ran and we won and he grinned and said, "You guys are good." We gave him half the track as a headstart, and that time we barely won. So we never gave him any more than that.

Finally Curly and I ran out of breath and decided to call it quits and go home. "See ya tomorrow, Bean," we yelled, our hearts pumping with the excitement of being the speed demons that we were. "Don't forget. You're in our gang now." Bean waved cheerfully.

After I crossed Apple Road I sat down on the big rock that marked the edge of our driveway. Something was wrong with Bean. But I didn't know what it was. The fun of winning all those races was fading away fast. I felt that I had done something to Bean that he didn't deserve. I wished I'd let him win a few races. I knew now he'd never be a basketball player. Somehow I knew he'd always be lagging behind through his whole life, just as he lagged behind in the orchard.

That night I said to Ta, "There's this boy in the orchard."

"Go on," said Ta.

"He's different. He's slow and he's not much good at anything except grinning."

"Go on," said Ta.

"He can't win at anything unless you let him win."

"Then let him win sometimes," said Ta. "For him to win is good for his heart. And good for yours, too."

12

I turned ten that summer. When school started Curly and I were in the fifth grade. Most of our orchard adventures had happened in the summertime. Summer days lay long and lazy and hot. Summer days begged for excitement. But ever since Jack and Willy and Chunk had joined the Willow Gang, they wouldn't let us alone. Even though school had begun, they wouldn't let us alone. The Willow Gang spent every spare minute baiting us and watching us and jeering us and chasing us. On weekdays from the afternoon school bell till supper was called. On Saturdays from dawn till dusk. Sundays, though, Curly and I had to stay home.

There were five of them altogether now in the Willow Gang counting Jack and Willy and Chunk and two older boys named Miller and Handy. There were just three of us. And it was really hard to count Bean as a one. He was more like a half because of his slow feet and slower thinking. On the other hand, I guess you had to count him as a two when it came to loyalty and good humor and willingness. But no matter how you counted Bean, it wasn't fair. The Willow Gang not only had more boys, they were older and bigger.

The apple leaves turned brown and fell off. The weeds dried up and got trampled down. One day Curly and Bean and I were playing Follow the Leader through a mound of leaves between the apple trees. That's when we saw the boot.

"Wonder who lost a boot," said Curly, who gave it a kick. The leaves shifted to show a leg attached to the boot. For once Bean didn't grin. Long and hard we stared at that leg. Then with the toe of my shoe I moved a few more leaves. It was a body! It was lying face down, and the upper half was still covered with leaves. I didn't want to move those leaves at all. I didn't want to see the face of a dead man. Or even the back of the head of a dead man.

"There's only one thing to do," I said. "We'll have to call the police. We can go over to the Pickly-Wickly. It's closest."

"I-I guess someone ought to stay here," said Curly. "I-I'll stay if Bean will." Bean nodded his head.

"Okay," I said. "Be right back." And I turned to run. I wanted to get out of there fast because I felt sick to my stomach. That's when we heard the crumpling and rattling of dry leaves. It was the Willow Gang coming.

"We been looking for ya," called Jack. "Whatcha doing?"

"We found something," I said, trying not to gag, not to look white, not to look green. The gang gathered round.

"Wow!" said Miller. "A body!" The minute Miller spoke, I knew something. But I didn't know what I knew.

"I was just going over to the Pickly-Wickly and call the police," I said.

"Boy," said Handy, "you'll be a hero—reporting a body and all that. Maybe you'll even get your picture in the paper!" Again I knew something. But what was it? Something didn't seem right.

"I wonder if we know the man," I said, playing for time.

"Ain't nobody missing from around this neighborhood," said Chunk.

"Maybe we ought to search his pockets," I said. I looked around at the Gang and my eyes stopped at Willy. If it were a trick of some kind, Willy would be the first one to give it away. "Willy, why don't you check that pocket there?" Willy's face got red. He leaned over and barely stuck two fingers in the pocket.

"Nothing in there, Ig," he said. But I could see his lips were pressed together like he was holding something in, and even his ears were red. I had to keep talking. I had to break Willy, somehow. I had to know if it was a trick.

"Do you really think a newspaperman will be here?" I asked Handy.

"That's the plain truth, Ig," he said. That's when I heard Willy's first giggle, and that's when I got my first clue. This wasn't a body! It was a newspaperman—a suit of clothes stuffed with newspapers!

"Wow!" I said, acting excited. "Come on, Curly and Bean. We'll go and call the police *and* the newspaper. The rest of you guys guard the body!" Curly and Bean and I took off in the direction of the Pickly-Wickly. I don't know how long the Gang stuck around because Curly and Bean and I went on home. I hope they waited a long, long time.

We counted that as one of our victories. But most of the time we were plain snookered and bedeviled. And I guess most of the time I looked pretty sober, maybe even scared, when I got home. Those were the times when Ma would say, "Ignatius, are you afraid? Why do you play there if you're afraid?" And I didn't for the life of me know why I went. Why didn't I just stay home? That would spoil their fun for sure. Especially if Bean and Curly would stay home, too. But I couldn't. I guess they couldn't either. Something pulled me there. I had to try to outwit the Gang, outscare them, outrun them. Life wasn't life without the heart pump-pumping as I leaped the ditch into the treacherous orchard.

They called me Ig-Pig. That made me sick. Then they started calling me a dirty Polack. That made me sicker. And I was sick of being dared to do things I knew weren't right or safe. Yet I envied the Gang. I envied them their recklessness and their power. They were kings of the orchard. And I just had to keep proving I could take whatever they poured to me. Then, maybe someday, I would be asked to be in the Willow Gang, too. I wanted to taste that power. I wanted to climb that rope ladder and sit above the apple trees.

Winter came, and Pie Creek froze over. I got wet shoes because Miller dared me to test the thickness of the ice. "You think shoes grow on trees?" said Ta. "They are like boards!" groaned Ma, when they finally dried out.

The first snow came, and Patch Path became a sled run. I got shoved into the blackberry brambles in a downhill race with Handy. I got my face washed twice in snow. I got hit with a rock hidden in a snowball. And Curly and Bean didn't do any better. Our sleds we found one day wedged high in three separate trees. A whole day it took to get them down.

We decided we had to think of a trick. A BIG trick. So BIG it would pay them back in one lump for all the things they'd done to us. I thought and thought. Curly thought and thought. And I guess Bean thought and thought. Finally Bean shook his head hopelessly. "I wish a big black bear would come and whup them good!" That was the longest sentence we'd ever heard Bean say.

"Yeah," said Curly. "But where we going to get the bear?"

That's when I saw the whole trick laid out like a map. "Bean! You did it!" I yelled, slapping him on the back. "You thought of the trick! The BIG trick!" Bean's grin was so wide I thought it'd split his head in two. I guess that was the first time Bean ever got credit for thinking up something. He sure felt proud.

"What trick?" said Curly.

"The mysterious pawprints of the big black bear," I said. And then I told them my plan.

I knew that I would need Ta's help. The question was, would Ta help? Would he help with a trick to be played on other boys? The only thing to do was to ask.

It was after Christmas. Ta loves Christmas. He was still singing, *"Cichy noc, swiety noc,* All is calm, all is bright." He was still remembering the smoked ham, the stuffed goose, the pickled mushrooms, the *barszcz,* the holiday *strucel,* and best of all the Christmas sausage. It had been extra good this year. He was in the cellar putting away the sausage-maker until Easter. He was in a very good mood.

"Ta," I said.

"So?" he said. There was no dilly-dallying with Ta. There was no use telling him that they called me a dirty Polack and washed my face in snow and put my sled in a tree. You didn't get sympathy from Ta. You got down to direct talk and got direct answers.

"I need some wood and nails to build a trick to play on the Willow Gang."

"A trick," said Ta, thinking it over. "Will this trick hurt them?"

"No, Ta."

"What is the trick?"

"It is a pair of wooden shoes, big ones, with claws made out of nails sticking out in front. There have to be straps across so I can wear them. The next fresh snow in the orchard, I'm going to be the first one there. And when I leave, the only footprints in the orchard will be the pawprints of a big black bear." I saw a little smile light Ta's eyes, and he nodded.

"I will help," he said. "We will saw the boards the right size. Then with my pocketknife I will carve them like paws." Right away we got busy in the cellar.

Bean and Curly came one day to see the finished

bear shoes. We tried them out in a half-melted gray snowdrift on the shady side of the house.

"Wow!" said Curly. Bean grinned.

"Now all we have to do is wait for a good snow," said Curly.

"What we want is a Friday night snow," I said. "Saturday morning would be the best time to find pawprints in the orchard. Then we'd have the whole day to stand around and laugh."

So we waited for the snow. It did not come. We prayed for the snow. It did not come. The sun shone all through January. The sun shone all through February. Folks were saying what a strange winter it was. What a good winter it was.

March was about the last month we could expect snow. My prayers were getting desperate. "Please, please, please," I kept saying to God. I even got to bargaining with God, though Father Janowicz said that God did not bargain. I promised to be nicer to my sisters. To sweep the sidewalks before I was asked. To stop throwing dirty socks under my bed. I even said to God one day, "God, if you'll just send us a Friday night snow, I'll get Father Janowicz a God window." Now, how I ever thought I could get Father a God window, I'll never know.

But the following Friday after supper, it began to snow. It was a light snow, like a little shake of Ma's flour sifter now and then. But when I went to sleep, it was still snowing.

It was dark yet when I felt someone shaking my shoulder. It was Ta.

"Big black bears have to get up early," was all he said. I put on my warm clothes and went outside, carrying the bear shoes under my arm. It was so early the streetlights were still on. A few cars had traveled Apple Road and I walked in the car tracks. I walked all the way down to Meister and up Meister a way before I put on the bear shoes. Then I stepped carefully into the orchard.

I had practiced in my mind a million times what I would do. I tried to make the same kind of tracks a four-footed animal would. At a narrow place in Pie Creek I broke the ice as if the big black bear had stopped to get a drink. Then I stepped across the creek, walked a crooked path around a few apple trees and made for the Willow. I circled the Willow Tree and with my fingers made scratches on the snow-covered trunk. Then I walked back to Meister, took off the bear shoes and walked toward home in a car track. The City streetlights blinked off just as I reached the porch.

Ta was in the kitchen when I got home. Ma and Felicia and Irka and Reka were still asleep. Ta set out two bowls and the box of cornflakes. He poured two mugs of coffee. After milking and sugaring mine good he handed it to me and winked. It was the first coffee I ever had. While we ate our breakfast, I told Ta exactly what I had done.

"If the trick works," Ta warned, "if the Willow Gang is really fooled, they will see only red."

"Mad as hornets," I said, and I couldn't help smiling. "Ta, I have to go. I have to be there when they come." Ta nodded.

I knew when Bean and Curly saw the snow, they would get up good and early. They were waiting for me at the corner of Apple and Pie. They were pacing up and down and rubbing their hands together to keep warm.

"No sign of them yet," whispered Curly. We didn't know just what to do with ourselves. We didn't want to seem suspicious just standing around waiting. Awful early it was, but we didn't want to miss a minute of what was going to happen. We fooled around trying to make a snowman near the culvert.

Jack was the first one to come along. He lives over on Hannibal and he had followed Pie Creek along the banks. He had a stick and was poking the ice. We could hear the crack-crack-crackle as he got nearer and nearer. Suddenly the crackling noises stopped and I knew he had seen the strange pawprints. We kept talking and laughing about our snowman, though, as if we didn't even know Jack was there.

It wasn't long till Chunk and Willy came charging along Meister and spotted Jack standing there by the creek. Jack whistled them over. We got quiet then. We just had to listen.

"Look what I found!" said Jack.

"Wow-ee!" said Chunk. "No little rabbit made them tracks!"

"What kind of animal could it be?" asked Willy.

"You mean you don't know!" said Jack. "Man, them are bear tracks! And some bear!"

"He must of got a drink here," said Chunk. "Are there still bears around these here parts?"

"Out in the country, maybe," said Jack. "This here bear must've got lost."

"Let's follow the tracks," said Willy.

"Yeah, but slow," said Jack. "He might still be in the orchard."

Their voices got farther and farther away as they followed the tracks I had made in and out among the apple trees. Then they turned back our way and stopped at the Willow.

"Look!" gasped Willy. "He sharpened his claws on our tree!"

"I bet he smelled us," said Chunk. "If we'd been up there, he'd have clumb up in a hurry. We'd of been his dinner!"

"He went back to the creek," said Jack, leading the way, "and over to Meister. Come on. Let's see where the tracks go."

It didn't take long for their voices to return. "He musta taken off straight down Meister. There's not a sign of pawprints on the other side of the street," said Jack.

"I wonder how he got here," said Willy.

"He could have escaped from a cage, maybe from a railroad car or something," said Chunk.

By that time Curly and Bean and I couldn't stand it anymore. We decided to walk over to the Willow where the boys were staring down at the mysterious tracks.

"What're you looking at, guys?" I said, in the nonchalant way Jack always had.

"Look at these pawprints, Ig!" said Willy. "Jack says they belong to a bear!" Curly and Bean and I studied the prints. They sure did look real. I could feel Jack's eyes on my back as I leaned over, and suddenly I knew what he was going to say. And I knew that I had to say it first.

"Hah!" I said. "You can't fool us. You made those pawprints and you're trying to scare us!"

I really caught Jack by surprise. He stood there with a puzzled frown on his face and bit his lower lip. Now he didn't know what to believe. Boy, I knew I had old Jack right where I wanted him.

He stuttered around a minute and then I about fell over in the snow when he said, "Yeah. You're right. I guess you caught me fair and square, Ig. I did it."

"Why didn't you tell Willy and me?" demanded Chunk.

"Well," said Jack, "I thought I'd fool everyone."

"But how did you do it?" I asked.

Jack stuttered around some more. "Well, I guess that'll have to be my little old secret."

"Pretty neat trick, Jack," I said. Then Bean and Curly and I lit out of there because we were about to burst laughing. We went right to my house and got the bear shoes. We took them to the upper orchard then and took turns wearing them and making bear tracks all over the place. We hollered and laughed and made plenty of noise so the Willow Gang would hear us.

Sure enough, they couldn't stay away. When they saw what we had and what we were doing, you should have seen their faces!

"We thought you said you did it, Jack!" said Willy and Chunk. Jack just stood there breathing hard and staring at our bear shoes. The big cheese sure had changed into a little cheese fast. Even Willy and Chunk looked at him for a minute like he was some little cheese.

"That's the trouble with having dumbbells like you in the Gang," said Jack, turning toward them. "You believe everything you're told!" And he ran off. Pretty soon Willy and Chunk left, too, and we didn't see any of them the rest of the day.

We made a great slide on Patch Path that day and gave all the little kids rides on our sleds. Boy, that was some day!

When I was walking home carrying the bear shoes and pulling my sled, I just happened, for no reason at all, to look up at the church. There was the plain round window above the High Altar. It was like a big eye looking at me. I remembered then the bargain I'd made with God. "Please send a Friday night snow," I'd said, "and I'll get Father Janowicz a God window." Boy, it was a good thing Father Janowicz had said that you couldn't bargain with God. It was a good thing that the snow just happened along at the right time and God didn't have anything to do with it. Or I'd be worrying myself sick about how to get a window for Father, a window with all the colors of the rainbow in it.

Jack was like a hot ash after that. He just stayed red and never burned out. I think way back then, when there was still snow on the ground, he started to think up the War. The Great Green Apple War. Of course, at the time we didn't know it. We did know that Miller and Handy didn't come around anymore and that Jack and Willy and Chunk asked Bean to join the Willow Gang. I guess even then Jack was counting up sides. That would make four on their side and two on ours for the Great Green Apple War.

14

The snow finally melted, and spring came around. My whole family and all the families of the Polish-in-America Church started to get ready for Easter. Easter is real big with us. There is lots of going to church. There is lots of good eating. Ma and Felicia and Irka and Reka started cooking two weeks before Easter. Ta got out the sausage-maker and made the sausage and smoked it in his little smokehouse. Tears rolled down his cheeks when he ground up the horseradish roots for the making of the Easter horseradish sauce. "Aí!" he said. "This will be the hottest sauce ever made in all of Poland and America, too!"

The day before Easter Ma laid out samples of all the things we'd be eating on Easter Sunday and Father Janowicz came and blessed the food. Oh, how my mouth watered! But I knew that not a bite could be eaten until after the big Easter Mass on Sunday morning.

While the last *alleluja* still hung in the air, I raced out the door of the church, ran across Apple Road, and grabbed a chunk of sausage and one of the eggs Ma had boiled with onion skins. There was a cake in the middle of the table molded in the shape of a lamb. And all around were plates and bowls and baskets of *babki* and rice *budyn* and *mazurki* and other good things to eat. And there were sprigs of green leaves to decorate the table. I guess the leaves showed that spring was here, that the Resurrection Day was here, that flowers would bloom and lambs be born and the world made new again. It was a happy, happy day.

Curly came over with Father Janowicz, and we had an egg contest to see who had the strongest egg. We would tap-tap them together, and the hard-boiled egg that didn't crack was the winner. You had to eat your cracked egg before you could challenge the winner again with another egg. I wonder how many eggs we ate that day. About a million.

After Easter the orchard turned into a flower garden with pink and white apple blossoms everywhere you looked. Felicia and Irka and Reka ohed and ahed and oohed the way they did every year. And whenever I went to the orchard I felt that I was in some girl place full of perfume and lace. But finally the blossoms fell to the ground, and the little green marbles of apples began to show among the leaves. Little did Curly and I know that the Great Green Apple War was drawing nearer. That is to say, until the day we saw Jack and Willy and Chunk and Bean picking green apples and putting them into grocery sacks.

"Why are they doing that?" wondered Curly.

"Yeah," I echoed. "Why are they doing that?"

"They're too sour to eat," said Curly.

"They sure couldn't sell them," I said.

"Heck, all they're good for is to throw," said Curly.

"At us," I said. Our eyes met. Would they really throw apples at us? A hard green apple might hurt more than a rock in a snowball. But Jack still had that look in his eyes ever since the bear tracks. We couldn't trust Jack. We hurried home to get grocery sacks and began to pick our own supply of apples in the upper orchard.

"Too bad we aren't knights," said Curly.

"Why?"

"A knight wears armor. Boy, a knight wouldn't even feel a green apple!"

"We could make shields," I said. "Even cardboard shields would help."

"Hey, yeah!" said Curly. "And I know where we can get some heavy cardboard. Mrs. Rakowski just got a new mattress, and it was in a big cardboard carton. Uncle Father helped her son unpack it and put it on her bed."

"I guess Mrs. Rakowski *is* going to live to be a hundred, just like Father Janowicz said."

"Yeah," said Curly. "She still thinks she's dying all the time though. I'll bet Uncle Father gets called every month."

We made ourselves two dandy shields out of Mrs. Rakowski's mattress carton. And I guess those shields probably saved our lives. One Saturday afternoon when we didn't see the Willow Gang around, we decided to practice with our shields in the orchard. That was when the Great Green Apple War started.

107

Lucky we were to have our shields with us because that's all we had. Our apples were stashed away at home. We had been afraid to try to hide them in the orchard. The Willow Gang might have found them. So there we were with shields and no ammunition except what we could pick on the run. We hadn't heard the Willow Gang come at all. Suddenly they were almost on top of us, firing apples like bullets out of machine guns. And yelling things as fast as they threw.

"You dirty Polacks, you!"

"We'll chase you out of this orchard forever!"

"Chickens! Chickens! Chickens!"

I suppose Bean wasn't yelling. But he was probably grinning and throwing as best he could. He'd be as loyal to the Willow Gang as he once was to Curly and me.

I guess Curly and I didn't have any choice, and we both knew it right away. We ran. We dodged like rabbits this way and that way, trying to escape the rain of apples. By the time we reached the upper orchard, the bullets had slowed down, and I wondered if the Willow Gang was running out of ammunition. I climbed one of the last orchard trees before the church property began. I wanted to pick some apples and get in a few good licks before Curly and I lost the War. It was hard to hang onto my cardboard shield and climb at the same time. I was just reaching up to pick an apple when I felt, or heard, one zing past my head. Boy, if that apple had hit me in the head, I'd have been a goner.

In the next second we heard it. The splintering of glass. That apple had gone right through the round church window above the High Altar. I turned around just in time to see Jack's hand still in the air and his mouth hanging open. Jack had thrown the apple, the little green apple that now lay somewhere in the Polish-in-America Church.

After that the Willow Gang disappeared like magic. I slowly climbed down, and Curly came out from behind a tree. We couldn't talk for a minute. We just stared at the broken window.

Finally I said, "Where's Father?"

"He's at your house," said Curly. "It's the monthly meeting of the Church Officers. I gulped. I knew that finally something had happened in the orchard important enough and serious enough to need telling right away. But I sure didn't look forward to telling it at a meeting of the Polish-in-America Church Officers. Our feet dragged as we crossed Apple Road.

"What'll we say?" asked Curly.

"I don't know," I said.

"Are we going to tell on Jack?"

I shrugged my shoulders. "Let me do the talking, Curly. Just back me up, will you?"

"Sure thing, Ig," said Curly with a sigh of relief. "Don't worry. I'll back you up."

The Polish-in-America Church Officers were sitting around our dining room table—Mr. Polanski and Mr. Rakowski and Mr. Pyrska and Father Janowicz and Ta. They were probably talking about money. They always talked about money. Where would the money come from to do this and to do that? Ma met Curly and me at the front door. "Go play," she said. "They are having the meeting now."

"We have to talk to them, Ma," I said. "It's important." I guess Ma could tell by our white faces that it was really important, and she opened the door. We went to the dining room. The Church Officers stopped talking and looked at us.

"Ah, boys," said Father Janowicz. "You come to learn how the Church is run. Someday you be the fine Officers of the Church. It is good that you have come to learn."

"Please, Father, we have something important to tell," I said.

"Is it about the Church, Ignatius?" asked Ta.

"Yes, Ta. There was a fight in the orchard. Green apples were thrown. One went through the round window above the High Altar."

Oi!" said Mr. Polanski. "More money now we need for a window! Money, money, money! Where will it end?"

"Who threw the apple, Ignatius?" asked Mr. Pyrska.

"It was my fault, Mr. Pyrska. I climbed a tree and the apple was aimed up high at me. That is why it went through the window."

"But who threw it, my boy?" asked Mr. Rakowski. I looked at Ta. How could I be respectful to Mr. Rakowski and yet not be a tattler?

"The name does not matter," said Ta. "The window is broken, and that is that. Ignatius takes the blame, and Ignatius will earn the money for a new window."

"I take the blame, too, sir," said Curly. "I was on Ig's side in the fight. I will earn money also to buy the new window."

"It is settled then," said Father Janowicz. "Is it

not settled, gentlemen?" They nodded their heads. "Then we go to the Church and see the damage. We board up the window till the boys buy the new one."

Curly and I followed the Church Officers across the road to the Church, wondering all the way how we could ever, ever, ever earn enough money to buy a round window for above the High Altar.

15

Curly and I worked. Man, did we work! After school and on Saturdays till school let out for the summer. And after that every day but Sunday. Sundays we sat under a tree or on the porch steps thinking up more work. We washed windows. We washed cars. We dug garden plots. We raked yards. We weeded. We mowed. We painted a garage. We ran errands. We dug dandelion greens and tried to sell them, but nobody wanted any.

Every day we got together and counted up our money. Father Janowicz had a church catalog with candlesticks and organs and altar cloths and pews and crucifixes and church windows in it. Even a small plain round window cost an awful lot.

We hardly ever saw the Willow Gang anymore. We didn't have time to set foot in the orchard except to use Patch Path as a short cut to get over to Hannibal. But we knew the Gang was there. Somehow or other we could feel their breaths on the backs of our necks when we hightailed it over to see Mr. Perrini. It was a queer thing—that power the Willow Gang had.

Every time Curly and I lifted our eyes to the place where the window was boarded over, we felt bad. It was worse inside the church on Sunday mornings. The High Altar seemed so very dark, even though there were lots of candles up there. And all around us sat the church members, knowing Curly and I caused the window to be broken. I could feel their eyes asking, "Where's the money for the new window? Are we going to sit in the dark forever?"

At last one day, after we'd made a dollar and eighty-four cents between us cleaning out Mrs. Rakowski's cellar, delivering a grocery order for Mr. Perrini at the Pickly-Wickly, and painting some porch steps for a Mr. Stanfield on Meister, we got out our peanut butter jar and dumped the money once again on Curly's bed. When we finished counting and had counted again to make sure, Curly threw a pillow at me. "We did it," he said. "We got enough money!"

I should have been one happy cookie, but for some reason I wasn't.

"See?" said Curly, pointing to a page in the catalog. "Right here it is. $15.95 and we've got enough for the tax, too!"

I stared at the picture in the catalog. And suddenly I knew why I wasn't happy. It had something to do with that Friday night snow. It had something to do with the bargain I'd made with God. "Give me snow," I'd said, "and I'll get Father a God window." Father Janowicz said God didn't bargain. Yet, when the plain round window had gotten broken, maybe God's hand helped Jack throw the apple. Maybe the window was meant to be broken. Maybe God was

114

testing me. I knew I just had to buy Father a God window, the one on the next page of the catalog, the one with all the colors of the rainbow that cost $37.95. But how could I tell Curly this? He wasn't the one who fooled around bargaining with God. It wasn't fair to him.

"Ig," said Curly, breaking into my thoughts. "We can't buy the plain round window. We have to buy this God window that costs $37.95."

I stared at Curly in surprise. I almost did a backward flip off his bed. Curly turned the page of the catalog and pointed to the picture. "This is our chance, Ig. Remember way back when we were little duffers and were trying to pick a million blackberries and get a million dollars for a God window? Well, we can finally do it and . . ."

"Yeah, Curly," I interrupted eagerly. "We don't have to tell anyone. No one knows we have enough money for a plain window. We'll just keep working and saving till we get enough for the window Father really wants. Maybe we'll have to work all summer long and never get to play. But we'll see the God window up there for the rest of our lives!"

We put the money back in the peanut butter jar. And we worked and we worked and we worked some more. And it seemed sometimes as though the God window could never be bought. We were so busy, I didn't even think about my birthday coming in July. One morning when I got up, there was Felicia stirring up the *baba* cake and Ma had made potato *placki* for my breakfast.

"Eleven years old already!" said Ma, shaking her head.

"Eleven candles on the *baba* cake!" said Felicia.

"Bet you can't blow them all out, Ig," said Irka.

"Don't worry. Mr. Big Wind can do it," teased Reka.

Curly and Father Janowicz came for my birthday supper. When Felicia came from the kitchen and put the *baba* cake in front of me, I looked around the birthday table at all the family smiling at me. The heat from the eleven candles made my chin warm. I was almost a happy cookie. But I couldn't help wondering what they were thinking. Just about the birthday? Or were they thinking that it was taking an awful long time to buy a plain round church window? That maybe Curly and I were lazy? That maybe we were spending some of the money for licorice whips or jawbreakers? Not one of them, not Father Janowicz either, had ever asked how much money we'd saved. It worried me.

I didn't see any birthday presents anywhere. But I guess when you are eleven, you do not look around like a little kid for presents. You just sit tall and polite.

"Under your plate," said Ma. "Look under your plate, Ignatius."

There lay an envelope, all sealed, with my name on the front. Slowly I opened it. Inside was a note: HAPPY BIRTHDAY, IGNATIUS, FROM FELICIA, IRKA, REKA, MA, AND TA. And inside was a piece of paper money. Ten dollars! I had never had a ten-dollar bill in my whole life! In my family we don't get big presents. Ma says, "We can just give little, but we love big."

"Wow!" I said. "Wow!" And then I couldn't say

anymore because my throat filled up with Pie Creek again the way it was always doing. I held up the money for Curly to see.

"What are you going to buy with your birthday money?" asked Felicia.

"Maybe he's going to spend it on a girl," teased Irka.

"Or buy a red convertible," teased Reka.

I swallowed and took a big breath. "Curly and I are going to buy a God window for the Church," I said. "We saved enough money a long time ago for a plain round window. But we didn't want just a plain one. We wanted one with all the colors of the rainbow in it. Now we have enough money." I looked across the table at Father Janowicz. I could see the flames of the birthday candles dancing in his wet eyes.

"Ah, boys," he said. "What a thing this is you do! A beautiful God window!" He fumbled for his big handkerchief and blew his nose. I guess I wasn't the only one with Pie Creek splashing inside of me.

"Ig!" yelled Curly. "Blow out the candles! The *baba* cake is going to burn!"

So I, Mr. Big Wind, Ignatius Zaska, blew out the candles and saved the *baba* cake and the whole house from burning down. And the next day, we sent off our money, $37.95 and the tax, for the beautiful God window. We had twenty-two cents left over for licorice whips. And we had the rest of the summer for playing in the orchard.

16

I guess Jack and Willy and Chunk and Bean must have missed us. They didn't say they did. But when they saw us in the orchard again, they didn't play any tricks. I guess Jack knew Curly and I had never tattled on him for breaking the church window. I guess he knew that Curly and I had bought the new window ourselves. Maybe not tattling on Jack was what made him decide we were tough enough to be in the Willow Gang.

One day there was a note on the Post Office Tree. TO IG AND CURLY: IF YOU WANT TO BE IN THE WILLOW GANG PUT YOUR FINGERPRINT IN BLOOD HERE. We pricked our fingers with a blackberry thorn and pressed the blood against the paper. We were so happy, our fingers didn't even hurt. We sat and sucked them till the bleeding stopped. I guess we looked like two Beans sitting there because our grins were so big.

So here I am now in the Willow being initiated. Here I am now high above the apple trees. As high as you can get in the orchard. The sky is getting light in the east. I sure feel stiff and sore. I don't know whether I spent the whole night sleeping and dreaming, or spent the whole night awake and remembering. I stretch and yawn. In the middle of my yawn I almost choke because out of the corner of my eye I see two feet. I turn around and there Curly is, stretched out fast asleep on the treehouse floor behind me. Then I remember that he came in the night to visit me.

"Curly, wake up!" I shake his shoulder. "Golly, Curly, you have to get out of here! What if the gang sees you! I'm supposed to be alone!"

Curly sits up and rubs his eyes. "It's almost morning!" I say. "The sky's getting gray! Does Father Janowicz know you're here? Wow, Curly! Maybe he's got the police out looking for you!"

"He knows I came to see you, Ig. Heck, he won't be worried. Guess we fell asleep, huh?"

I nod my head.

"Guess the gang never came back in the night. Did you hear them, Ig?"

"Nope." I stand up then and look around. The orchard is coming alive. It's beginning to sing its daytime song, and the nighttime music-makers are crawling back into their beds. Everything is getting clearer. I can see Patch Path now, for sure, and the Northern Spy and the blackberry bushes and Tree Cave Number One and the Post Office Tree and Pie Creek and the culvert. I stretch my arms out like I am the fellow who owns it all. This is the place for me! This is my orchard, my land, my world!

"What are you doing, Ig?" asks Curly.

"I don't know. Feeling power, I guess. Just think, Curly, we're going to be top bananas! We're going to be in the Willow Gang! This orchard will be ours. There's not one thing going on in the orchard that we won't . . ."

That is when my voice stumbles like it tripped over a tree root. I stare at the corner of the orchard near Hannibal. There is the bulldozer, the mysterious bulldozer. Its bright orange paint is saying, "See me, see me," as the sky gets lighter. Curly stands beside me and we look at it together. I try to wrap my mind around it. If I think hard enough, maybe I'll figure out why it's there.

"They use bulldozers when they build roads," says Curly. I nod in agreement.

"Bulldozers push the dirt around to make the roads level," I nod again.

"Bulldozers shove everything out of the way, like bushes and trees."

That's when the goosebumps hit me. "Apple trees," I say. "They shove over old wormy apple trees!"

"But why?" gasps Curly.

"To make room for marking off lots and building houses."

Curly groans. "They can't do that to us!" he says, pounding both his fists against a limb of the Willow tree. "It's robbery!"

I wish I could get mad like Curly and stamp around and pound my fists. All my madness stays inside. It's like a Great Green Apple War tearing me apart. I can't seem to get enough breath.

"What'll we do, Ig? We gotta do something!"

moans Curly. "Gosh, Ig—Ig, don't you even care?"

"I care! I care!" I yell, and the yelling feels good. It surprises Curly and it surprises me. "We just have to think," I say in a calmer voice.

"If we had some dynamite we could blow up the old bulldozer!" says Curly. "Man, I'd just like to see that! A million orange pieces falling down on the orchard. Or if we could just hide it somehow, so they could never find it in a million years!"

"We can't blow it up, Curly. We don't have any dynamite. And we can't hide anything *that* big. But we gotta do something. Something that'll give us time."

"What do you mean—time?" asks Curly.

"Time maybe to get up a petition or see the mayor or something like that. And I think I know how to do it," I say slowly, still thinking out my idea.

"How?"

"We can get some tools and take the bulldozer apart."

"Hey, yeah! Wow! That's some idea!"

"We gotta do it now! We can't waste any time. They may be coming today to start shoving over the trees. Come on! We'll borrow Ta's tools."

"But what about the Willow Gang? They'll be mad as heck when they come and find you're not here."

"Curly! This is more important. We'll be saving the orchard for them!" I grab the rope and slide to the ground. Curly is right behind me.

We zigzag between the trees and come out on Apple Road just in time to see Ta walk down the driveway and head toward the bus stop.

"Wait, Ta. Wait!" I yell. But Ta doesn't hear me.

Part of me wants to run after Ta and tell him about the bulldozer and ask him what to do. The other part wants to hide until Ta disappears and then run to the house and grab his tools without asking. There I stand with my two parts fighting each other until Ta's bus comes. He climbs on and I give a big sigh. Now I don't have to decide because there is only the one thing left to do. Curly and I head for the house and scurry down the cellar stairs. We get wrenches and pliers and the biggest screwdriver Ta has and two hammers, and we start toward the orchard.

The closer we get to the bulldozer, the slower my feet want to go. Curly is calling me to hurry, but I can't. It seems like my sneakers are made of concrete. My mind begins to ask a whole bunch of questions it didn't have time to ask before. Who owns the bulldozer? What will the owner do when he sees it in pieces? Will he call the police? What will Ta say, and what will Father Janowicz say? Will the mayor listen to two boys? What if someone is watching us right now?

My heart begins to pound at the thought. I look all around, but no one is in sight. I almost bump into the bulldozer I am so busy looking. The bulldozer looks ten times bigger down here than from the treehouse. It is an orange monster. I already hear Curly hammering away on the other side. I start walking around it, trying to see how it is put together. The nuts and bolts are giant-sized. Some parts are riveted together. I look at that orange monster, and then I look down at the small tools in my hand.

Just then Curly comes around from the other side. His face is all red, and sweat is rolling down the edges of his hair. "We can't do it, Ig," he says. "We can't do it nohow!"

I already know it. Not in a million years can we take apart this bulldozer with these tools. Part of me wants to laugh out loud with relief, and the other part wants to sit down and bawl.

Just then Jack's angry voice calls from the treehouse. "Hey, you dirty Polacks, I thought you wanted to be in the Willow Gang! What's the matter, Ig? Too chicken to spend the night alone in the orchard?"

"If you had a brain, Jack, you could figure it out," I yell. That brings Jack and the rest of the gang in a hurry. They scuttle down the rope ladder, and in two shakes Jack is waving his fist in front of my nose.

"Take it easy, Jack," I say, and I tell him about the bulldozer—how it's going to start pushing down trees, how they're going to come and mark off lots, how they'll start digging cellars and building walls and putting on roofs. How there won't be an orchard anymore.

Jack and Chunk and Willy and Bean look at me in disbelief. "Aw, you're nuts, Ig!" snarls Jack. But I watch his eyes rove around the orchard and then back to the bulldozer and I can tell that they think it's going to happen, too.

"We were trying to stop them," says Curly. "But we can't."

"Yeah," mutters Jack, looking at our tools. "That was a dumb idea! But I'll think of something," he adds, his voice cracking. "I just gotta. I gotta!" And he turns his back to us. He leans his hand against a tree trunk and looks off toward the church like he's thinking. We all wait for him to say something, but he doesn't. So after awhile, Curly and I gather up the tools and start toward my house. We haven't gone far when we hear Jack's voice calling after us, "Yer in the Willow Gang now—both of ya."

Curly nudges me. "Well, we finally made it," he says.

"Yeah," I say. "Big deal! Too late."

I sit on the front steps and wait for Ta. It is time for him to be getting home from the rubber factory. It seems like a million years have gone by since yesterday. Yesterday I was sitting right here and worrying about how to get permission to sleep in the orchard for initiation. And now today I'm a member of the Willow Gang. But there isn't going to be a Willow Tree, so how can there be a Willow Gang?

The bus stops at the corner, and Ta gets off with his lunch pail and his evening paper. I guess he knows I've been waiting for him because he sits beside me on the top step.

"Ta, there's a bulldozer in the orchard."

"A bulldozer?"

"Ta, it's going to knock down the apple trees and the Willow Tree. It's going to take the orchard away from us!"

Ta nods.

"Maybe, it's just parked there for awhile, Ta. Maybe they're going to take it on up Hannibal for some roadwork. Do you think so?"

Ta unfolds the newspaper. "It tells in here, Ignatius. They are going to build apartment houses in the orchard."

"Oh! Can we get the mayor to stop them?"

"I think not, Ignatius."

"But there can't be a Willow Gang without a Willow Tree and an orchard!"

"Can't there? Maybe it is time for the orchard to end—time for the Willow Gang to do new things."

"Like what, Ta?"

"There will be many men and machines in the orchard."

"You mean they'll need helpers, Ta?"

"Maybe."

"And there'll be new kids moving in, lots of new kids, won't there, Ta?"

"Lots," agrees Ta. "Maybe enough for a baseball team and a football team."

"I-I sure hate to see them cut down the Willow, though. And, Ta, it won't ever be the same again."

"I know, Ignatius." Ta stands. He leans over and rumples my hair and then walks up the steps and into the house.

Ma calls me for supper, but I don't feel like eating. I just sit there and watch the shadows of the orchard trees get longer and longer. After awhile the lightning bugs start winking among the branches. The crickets start creaking, and the frogs start grumping. I close my eyes and try to see apartment houses across the road in the orchard. But I can't. I just can't.

The End